Not a laughing matter

Case watched in horror as a photocopy of *Dog Years* floated from Tyler's notebook to Ms. Riley's big feet. She scooped up the paper and read it intently. The whole class was silent.

"Mr. Hill. My desk, please." Case stood up slowly and walked the short distance. She pointed dramatically at *Dog Years*.

"It's my comic for English class," Case said.

"I know what it is, Mr. Hill. I thought I told you I didn't need any more disruptions in my class."

But I didn't bring it, Case thought wildly, glancing for a second at Tyler. Tyler was twisting a pencil back and forth, back and forth, and didn't look at Case.

Case forced himself to look back at Ms. Riley. "I'm sorry," he said simply.

"Sorry's not good enough, not in middle school," Ms. Riley said. "I'm going to have to confiscate this. That means I keep it."

A Knopf Paperback by the same author:

Some Friend

Dog Years

SALLY WARNER

A Knopf Paperback
Alfred A. Knopf
New York

For Stuart Warner, with love and gratitude

A KNOPF PAPERBACK PUBLISHED BY ALFRED A. KNOPF, INC.

http://www.randomhouse.com/

Library of Congress Cataloging-in-Publication Data
Warner, Sally. Dog years / by Sally Warner.
p.   cm.
Summary: After his father is imprisoned, twelve-year-old Case switches to
a new school, where he makes some important discoveries about friendship
and honesty.
[1. Friendship—Fiction. 2. Schools—Fiction. 3. Honesty—Fiction.
4. Prisoners—Fiction.] I. Title
PZ7.W24644Do   1995
[Fic]—dc20   94-25457

ISBN 0-679-87147-0 (trade)
ISBN 0-679-88553-6 (pbk.)

First Knopf Paperback edition: May 1997
Printed in the United States of America
10 9 8 7 6 5 4 3 2 1

Reprinted by arrangement with Alfred A. Knopf, Inc.

★ CONTENTS ★

September 22

Dear Dad,

Hi! Well, school in Philadelphia is going okay, I guess. It's more interesting than in Cherry Hill. I told you about my friend Ned, he and I take the bus together. I like my teachers okay except Ms. Riley, but that's just homeroom. It's short. We're going to make a newspaper in English. That's the class I like best. I'm making some bucks after school, I work in a store. I help out. Lily is fine, she misses you. She likes first grade a lot and thinks she knows everything now. Mom is fine, she likes working at the bookstore. I hope you got the car magazines I sent. Did you? They looked pretty good. We'll come see you soon, Mom says there is a family day around Thanksgiving so that's not too long. Write and say what you want us to bring, what food. I hope you are fine, not too bored. Maybe I'll send you our class newspaper if it ever comes out, ha ha! If you get a chance to write, make it to Lily first because it's hardest for her.

Your son,

Case

DOG YEARS

"I'm older than you in dog years, Case," Lily said after dinner. She and Casey were at the kitchen table. Case had just finished writing a letter to his father and was trying to work on his English assignment. Ms. Yardley was the one teacher he liked at his new school, and he wanted to do a good job for her. Lily sat watching him. She banged her sneaker against the chrome leg of the kitchen chair. "I am," she said, smiling, as her brother looked up and sighed.

"What do you mean, you're older than me?"

"In dog years. Get it, Case? One year in people years is the same as seven in dog years. You know Champion, downstairs? Well, he's six in people years, but Buddy told me Champion's really forty-two." Buddy was their downstairs neighbor, and their landlord, too. His beautiful dog, Champion, loved the Hills, especially Case, who often took him for walks. "You times your age by seven to get dog years," Lily went on. "You need a calculator, though."

"No, you don't, Lily. You just need to learn your times tables."

"Oh sure, Case. What about if a person is twenty-five? No one can times twenty-five and seven."

Case gave up trying to explain multiplication to his stubborn little sister. Instead he asked, "How does that make you older than me?"

"In *dog years*. Get it? You're twelve, and I'm six, but in dog years I'm really forty-two, like Champion. Buddy told me. So that makes me older. I could be your mom, Case!" She grinned at him.

Case thought Lily looked like a Halloween jack-o'-lantern with her missing front teeth, but he didn't say so. He knew Lily would have a tantrum if she heard that. Her temper had gotten even worse since their father had been sent away. Case twiddled his pencil and said, "Lily, if I'm twelve in people years, then in dog years I'm..." He scowled and fumbled under the table with his fingers, trying to come up with the right number. "I'm eighty-four, I think. So in dog years, I'm still exactly twice as old as you."

"No, not twice as old! Not always! Anyway, I'm the only one who gets to be in dog years. You have to stay in people years," Lily said, her voice rising. "So that makes me older. It does!"

Case didn't answer her right away, because he was thinking. His sister had made him curious. "Well, you're right about one thing, Lily. I won't always be twice as old as you. When you were just one and I was seven, I was seven times older than you."

"No!" she howled.

Quickly, he went on. "But, Lily, listen. When you're... when you're twenty, I'll only be twenty-six. That's not twice as old," Case continued, excited. "It'll be shrinking, kind of. The difference, I mean."

"Who cares?" Lily shouted, making a face. "We'll be grown-ups then." She covered her ears and started to hum, loud, so he couldn't answer.

Case was used to this and turned back to his homework. Lily was still humming when the front door opened and their mother walked in, balancing a pink plastic laundry basket on one hip. The old washer and dryer the Hills used were in the basement of the house, down two steep flights of stairs. Case looked at his mother's tired face and gritted his teeth. Lily stopped humming and ran over to her.

"Mommy," she cried, "Case is trying to mix me up. On purpose!"

"No, I'm not, Mom."

"He said we were shrinking when we get older!"

"Shrinking?" Mrs. Hill smiled a little, looking at Case.

"The difference in our ages, Mom. I mean..." He didn't know how to explain what he meant.

"It will always be the same six years, Case," his mother said.

"See?" Lily said. "And in dog years, I'm forty-two. No matter what, I'll always be older. Get used to it, Case!" She stormed out of the kitchen and ran into the bathroom, slamming the door behind her. The bathroom was her favorite hideout.

Case and his mother looked at each other and burst out laughing. "Shhh!" Mrs. Hill said, waving her free hand at Case. She set the laundry basket on the table. Case could smell the clean, warm clothes from where he sat. "I don't want this squabble getting any worse than it already is. What on earth is going on, anyway?"

"Oh, Buddy told her about dog years. How Champion is really forty-two."

"I always wondered why that dog seems so much smarter than the rest of us," his mother said, and she laughed.

Case grinned back. "I guess Lily figures that since she and Champion are both six, they should both get to be forty-two dog years old."

"Makes sense, in a weird way. She's getting

tired of being the baby. I keep forgetting she's in school now! Which reminds me, young man, how's your homework going?"

"Not so good. We're supposed to make up an article, like for a newspaper. Whatever we want. This one guy is doing a sports thing, and Ellie, that girl who sits next to me, is writing about school politics. There's going to be a class election. She's already finished, I bet. She's always the first one done with every test, every paper, everything."

"Well, what's your idea for an article?"

Case shrugged. "I don't have one. I was trying to do something funny, like I thought of a fake cooking column with gross recipes and stuff. But that would just be good once, and Ms. Yardley wants us to keep writing these all semester, once she approves our topics."

"What about a gardening column?" Case's mother loved gardens and missed her old garden in New Jersey a lot. Back in Cherry Hill they had lived in a house of their own with a big yard attached. But in Philadelphia, the Hills didn't have even a tiny yard or a balcony for plants.

Mrs. Hill had brought two potted geraniums with them when they'd moved that last June. It made Case sad to look at them, and the dusty smell of their leaves made him feel sick.

"No, Mom, a gardening column wouldn't even be funny once."

"Do you have to be funny?"

Case balanced his pencil on his index finger. "I have to be *something*, Mom. I really wanted to do a pretend obituary column. You know, one that lists dead guys? Grandpa told me once newspapers used to say, 'Call Miss Black for sympathetic help with your obituary.' I could be 'Mr. Black.' "

Mrs. Hill laughed. "Your grandpa was a real character! But I think when it's time for your obituary, it's too late to call anyone. Even sympathetic Miss Black." His mother added, "Anyway, that's kind of depressing, don't you think?"

"I know, that's just what Ms. Yardley would say. It's too bad, though. I know I could make it funny."

"Thank goodness the obituary column is out. What other choices are there? Hmm...what about an advice column, like Dear Abby? You could be Dear Casey! You could make up people with unusual problems or even get your friends in the class to write in."

"I don't know any of them that well yet," Case said. He didn't want to add that he didn't *have* any friends in that class—or in any of his classes. Not counting Ned. But Ned was another story—and another problem, really. And his mom was worried enough about him already, he thought with a sigh.

His mother tried to cheer him up. "Case, it's still only September, and you're a new kid in a new school. These things take a while, honey."

"I guess. But I like the column idea, Mom," he said, trying to get her off the subject of friends. He thought a moment. "Maybe a fake gossip column?" he asked.

"Gossip? Would middle school kids be interested in that kind of thing?"

"Are you kidding? That's *all* they're interested in, practically. There's barely time for classes. But I'd make everything in the column up, just to be on the safe side."

His mother laughed. "That's smart. No point stirring up trouble." She stretched wearily, then smiled. "This is really bringing back the old days for me! There's probably enough gossip going on already, if school is anything the way I remember it. It's funny," she continued, "I remember when I was in junior high, some things happened we just couldn't get enough of. Every second was interesting. But then other times each minute dragged on until it seemed like ten minutes, and every hour felt like ten hours. It was as if you were going to be stuck in that year forever."

"Yeah," Case said, tapping his pencil thoughtfully against the Formica tabletop. He knew *he* was trapped in one of those years: His dad had been sent away to prison, they'd had to move, and then, on top of everything else, Case had started sixth grade at a new school. So far he hated it all, and it seemed as though every day was going to last a lifetime. But it was strange to think his mother had ever felt the same way.

"Maybe it's like some years are just dog years for everyone," he finally said to his mom. "They last extra long, and there's nothing you can do about it. Hmm..." He started to doodle on a blank sheet of notebook paper, ignoring the pale blue lines.

As he drew, a tiny voice came from the bathroom: "Isn't anybody going to say they're sorry?"

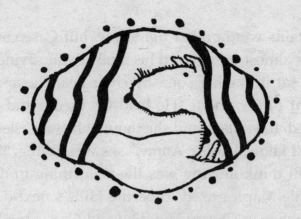

SUCH A
PASSIVE KID

Case didn't have a real room of his own anymore, but he had made a kind of cave for himself in a little alcove at one end of the apartment's main room. There was only space for his bed and a small painted table where he kept his favorite books and his clock radio. Green numbers from the clock glowed in the dark.

Right after they had moved to the city, Case's mother made red-and-white striped curtains for him to pull across the front of the alcove when he wanted privacy, which was most of the time. The curtains were pulled tight now, but Case could hear almost every word his mother was saying as she sat in the big squashy chair near the apartment's only phone. He held his breath and listened. It was late, and she thought he was asleep.

"I know, I know, Annie," she was saying. "But I still think moving was the right thing to do." Annie Maples used to be the Hills's next-door neighbor in Cherry Hill. She and Case's mother still talked on the phone almost every week.

There was a pause, then Mrs. Hill spoke again. "He says he's doing fine, but you know Dennis. Who knows what it's really like? I guess he'll get used to it, though. He'd better, since he'll be there at least three years. Robbery is no joke— thank goodness that truck driver wasn't hurt, that's all I can say. Anyway, Dennis calls a couple of times a week. Well, more like once a week, lately, mostly to talk to the kids. There's this pay phone they let the men use. Notice I say talk *to* the kids, not talk *with* them. No surprise there. He barely lets them get a word in. Case, anyway. It's hard to shut Lily up, even for Dennis." She gave a funny laugh. "He's still trying to manage everyone's life, even from prison. The kids' lives, at least. I guess he's given up on me."

She listened some more, then said, "Oh, they're okay, I guess. All things considered. School's started. That helps. But to be honest, Lily's acting up worse than ever. Lately, everything with her is slamming doors and shouting. It's almost as if she blames me for it all, when I was about the last one to know."

After another pause she said, "Well, Casey's...Casey is Casey. It's hard to tell what he's thinking. And he's such a passive kid these days. He's almost like a ghost! Just barely there. And he seems to just wait for things to happen to him. Won't call his old friends, and he's only made one new friend—that I know of, at least. I mean, he goes off to school every day and helps take care of Lily, and all. He's no problem, really. But he's taken this whole thing really hard, I guess."

She was silent for a little while, then spoke again. Her voice was firm. "I appreciate the offer, Annie. Really. But I don't feel like coming back just yet, even for lunch. Maybe you can come here for dinner? Well, think about it. I know the kids would love to see you again."

Maybe you *would*, Case thought. He didn't want any reminders of Cherry Hill, though. He flopped over to face the wall and pulled his pillow tight around his ears so he could get some sleep.

"When's Daddy coming home?" Lily asked the next morning between big spoonfuls of oatmeal. She asked this question almost every morning.

"Not for a long time," her mother said, still reading the paper.

"But how long?" Lily persisted. "Will it be when I'm still six?"

"Lily, you know it won't be for a long time," her mother repeated.

"But I'll be six for a long time," Lily pointed out, dog years forgotten.

Case interrupted. "Lily, Dad won't be home until you're at least nine, and probably not even then."

"Shut up, Case! I'm talking to Mommy. Right, Mommy?"

"Case is just trying to explain." Mrs. Hill looked up from the paper and sighed. "Lily, I wish we didn't have to start out this way every morning. Talking about your father."

"Yeah, Lily. It's depressing," Case said.

"It is not, it's fun!" Lily's eyes narrowed angrily as she looked at her brother. "You just want to forget all about him."

"No, I don't. Anyway, how could I?" Case asked, looking around the shabby apartment. He took a quick, guilty look at his mother, then swallowed a bite of cereal.

"Lily, no one wants to forget him," Mrs. Hill said soothingly. "We're not going to forget about him."

"We will if we don't talk about him." Lily's eyes filled with tears. "Maybe that's part of our punishment!"

"What is?"

"Forgetting." The tears spilled over.

"Lily," Case said, "stop crying. We're not the ones being punished. Dad is the one who robbed that truck. He stole a lot of things, Lily, all those video cameras. That's why he got sent to jail. He's the one doing time, not us."

"It was those other guys' fault, those guys he

was with! But our daddy got sent to jail, and we got sent to Philadelphia."

"Baby! I thought you liked it here," her mother said, pulling Lily onto her lap.

"I want my daddy," Lily sobbed. Case pushed his bowl of oatmeal away.

"Case, eat. You need a good hot breakfast, honey."

"Ned's waiting, Mom. I don't want us to miss the bus. Anyway, I'm full." Case grabbed his lunch sack and stuffed it into an already bulging backpack.

"You have your milk money? And your bus pass?"

"Got it, got it," Case mumbled.

And the ghost vanishes, he thought, as he ran down the stairs.

CASE AND NED

Ned was leaning against a wall, trying not to look anxious. It was a losing battle, since he always looked kind of nervous. His jacket was a little too big, and his pants were too short, as usual. Nothing ever really fit Ned, Case sometimes thought. And that was a funny thing, since Ned looked so ordinary. It should be easy for him to find clothes that fit.

Ned's thin face brightened with relief when he saw Case approach. "It's late!" he said.

"I know, I know. Sorry," Case said.

"No, I mean the *bus* is late, so we're okay." As he spoke, a city bus wheezed around the corner and squeaked to a stop in front of them. Ned scanned the interior of the bus and reported, "We get to sit today."

When they had settled back into the hard plastic seats, Case looked at his watch: It usually took them twenty-three minutes to get to school. There wouldn't be time to go to his locker before homeroom, and Ms. Riley didn't like kids bringing backpacks into her class. He sighed, then turned to Ned. "Hey. How would you define the word 'passive'?"

Ned pushed his glasses back with a long forefinger and smiled. He loved puzzles of any kind. Sometimes Case suspected Ned even liked homework.

"'Passive...' let's see. Well, it's the opposite of 'active,'" Ned began.

"So it's the same as what—lazy?"

"I don't think so. Not exactly." Ned never liked to say Case was wrong. "I think it's more like...more like sitting back. Going along with stuff, instead of making stuff happen."

"So if a person is passive, he's, like, a wimp?"

Ned chewed his lower lip. "Not necessarily. He could be, I guess. But he could just be more...passive."

Case poked Ned's ribs with his elbow. "Thanks a lot," he said. "That's like saying big is the opposite of little, and it means big."

Ned shrugged, happy to be teased by Case. "Sorry. But why do you want to know? You have a vocabulary test coming up?"

"Huh? Oh, yeah," Case said. There was no test, but he could get away with the fib, since he and Ned didn't have any classes together.

In fact, the two of them didn't really have very much in common at all, Case realized, except for living in the same neighborhood and hanging out together. They had met about two months before, shortly after the Hills had moved to Philadelphia. Case had been walking Champion, and Ned was walking Lacy, his grandmother's yappy little dog. They had ended up talking.

Ned lived alone with his granny in an old narrow house that faced a little park near the river.

He didn't know where his father was, but his mother lived in Texas. Case didn't know why Ned and his mother lived apart. He hadn't asked yet. They didn't talk about personal things much. He thought about himself and Ned: friends at home, strangers at school. He and Ned didn't talk about that, either.

Case knew Ned's grandmother was a worrier, though, and it was hard for him to get out of the house unless he was going to school, walking Lacy, or visiting the Hills. That meant he couldn't stay after school for clubs or team sports, like other kids. Ned didn't complain much, but Case knew how glad he was to have finally made a friend. Case hadn't been trying to make friends. It had just happened.

To Case's surprise, it had turned out to be a good summer after all. First he'd met Buddy Haynes, then he'd been offered a part-time job at the antique shop near his house, and then he'd made friends with Ned. It was true Ned was quiet, but he could be funny. When school had started, though, Case remembered what Ned had once predicted: He'd said, a little sadly, that it would probably be easy for Case to make friends.

Ned had gone to elementary school for two years already with many of the kids who were now at Ben Franklin, and they'd had plenty of time to decide he was weird. Case suspected Ned knew they felt this way.

Much to his relief, no one seemed to think Case was weird—in fact, no one noticed him much at all. Case felt like the invisible man at school, and he liked it that way. If people didn't notice him, maybe they would never find out about the robbery.

For Case and Ned, the morning bus ride was the only time they had together during the week. Case was eager to show Ned his latest project. "Hey," he said, "want to see something? It's for English." He rummaged in his backpack for a sheet of paper, then handed it to Ned. It was his third try, and it still wasn't exactly right, but it wasn't bad.

Ned smiled, then tilted his head and pointed. "What's this guy saying?"

"It's supposed to be a dog, not a guy. He's kind of the star of the comic strip. It's for the newspaper in Ms. Yardley's class."

"I think you spelled 'every' wrong. It's kind of

hard to tell, with all these smears."

Case snatched the comic back. "It's just a rough idea," he said. "Anyway, the important thing is the drawing, not the words."

"But I thought it was for English. Isn't it supposed to be writing?"

"It's more like creative writing," Case said. "You don't have Yardley. It's hard to explain."

"This *is* creative," Ned said, anxious to please his friend. "It's real creative, Case!"

"I just wish I could get the lettering better," Case admitted. "It's making my drawing look bad."

"I could help, if you want. If you do another one," Ned said cautiously. "I'm okay at lettering," he continued.

"Oh, come on, Ned. You're great at lettering." It was true. The inside of Ned's notebook was covered with different styles of lettering. His handwriting was good, too—much better than Case's.

"Thanks!" Ned's face turned sunny.

Case had an idea. "It'd be great if you'd do the lettering. As long as I always get to write the words. It's my project." He spoke fast, before he could change his mind about making the offer. He wanted to make Ned happy.

"Sure. I can be like your assistant."

"My *secret* assistant," Case corrected. "Or else it would be too hard to explain to Ms. Yardley."

"Thanks!" Ned repeated, his eyes shining. "What are you going to call the comic, Case?"

"The title's right up here. See?" Case pointed out.

"Uh, what's it say? This bus is kind of bumpy. It's hard to read."

"The comic's called *Dog Years*."

"*Dog Years*," Ned said to himself, as if trying out the words. "I like it."

The bus stopped just down the block from Ben Franklin Middle School. Kids pushed around Case and Ned as they stepped off the bus. Some looked serious, lost in thought, while shouts from others filled the cold morning air. The eighth graders towered over most of the other kids.

Two big eighth-grade boys shoved each other, calling names. Case and Ned gave them plenty of room as they walked toward the school's battered front doors. Then, without speaking, each went his own way.

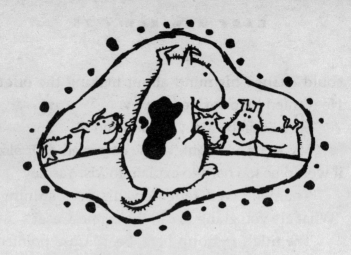

COMING INTO FOCUS

A few minutes after Case sat down in homeroom, he no longer considered himself the invisible man at Ben Franklin. "Mr. Hill!" Ms. Riley snapped, when she had finished reading the day's bulletin to the class.

"Yes, ma'am?"

"If there's any more noise from your corner, there's going to be trouble. Big trouble. *Detention* trouble."

Case slumped in his seat and tried to slip the

comic strip back into his notebook. This was the first time Ms. Riley had even spoken his name, except for taking roll. He knew he was blushing. He was actually in trouble, Case thought, amazed. And there was no way he could stay late for detention—he had to be at Mrs. Donovan's shop by four.

The kids sitting near Case had noticed *Dog Years* when he sneaked it out of his notebook during roll. He had wanted one last look at it before showing it to Ms. Yardley next period. But everyone around him wanted to see the comic strip too. They'd liked it! Now they busied themselves with imaginary work, trying to avoid their homeroom teacher's attention. Case didn't look up, but he sensed she was heading his way. The room was silent.

Now she was standing next to his desk. "Is that your backpack under your seat, Mr. Hill?" she began ominously. Case looked down at her feet. He could see big toes poking out of each shoe. Ms. Riley was wearing toenail polish! Case was so surprised, he dropped his felt-tip pen. When he reached down to get it, the teacher yanked the comic strip from his notebook and stared at it. "What's this?"

"It's—it's for English," Case stammered.

"English?" Ms. Riley squinted at the comic's title. The whole class watched her. School had only started a couple of weeks earlier, but the homeroom kids already knew it was hard to predict her actions. Ms. Riley always thought the kids in class were making fun of her—and so they did. *"Dog Ears?"* Ms. Riley asked, frowning.

"Years," Case said. *"Dog Years."* He could barely keep from grabbing it out of her hands. Just in time, the bell rang. But Ms. Riley blocked Case's way as the other homeroom kids streamed from the class, still quiet. She fanned the comic back and forth in front of her face, as if trying to decide what to do with it.

Finally, reluctantly, she handed the comic to Case. "Take it easy, Mr. Hill. I have a job to do here at Ben Franklin, and you aren't making it any easier for me."

"Yes, ma'am," Case repeated, but he felt as though his feet were frozen to the floor. He didn't think he could make his legs move, anyway.

Ms. Riley smiled a little and said, "You're free

to go. But no more backpacks in homeroom, and no more disrupting my class. Got the picture?"

His English teacher liked *Dog Years* a lot. Ms. Yardley was short, and bouncy with energy. Even her hair looked energetic. She wore it pulled back from her face with an elastic headband, but behind that her hair sprang out in curls, like a dark halo. "It's not what I had in mind for the assignment, exactly, and it needs work," she said during Case's meeting with her that morning, "but I can see it." Each student had a couple of minutes alone with the teacher while the other kids read. Ben Franklin Middle School called that Sustained Silent Reading. It seemed to Case they had a name for everything.

"I know your style is meant to be informal," Ms. Yardley continued, "but Casey, I can't even read some of these words. And I'm pretty sure you spelled 'every' wrong. It's kind of hard to tell with all these blobs of ink."

"I've worked out how to improve the lettering," Case said eagerly, not mentioning Ned.

Ms. Yardley went on: "And the cartoons have to reflect school life somehow, sixth-grade life especially. Think you can do that?"

Case nodded, silent.

Ms. Yardley nodded back at him, and every curl bounced. Some kids in the first row looked up at them. "Good," she said. "I think you can too, but you'll have to keep your eyes and ears open. Do you think you can do it for an entire semester, Casey?"

Case was thrilled. "I'm pretty sure I can," he said.

"Well, let's give it a try, then. It'll liven up our paper. I'll tell you the exact size to work in, and you'll have to turn in your comic on time, no excuses. We'll be counting on you."

"Okay!" Case said.

"Fine, then. This is Friday, and we'll need your first comic—with nice *clear* lettering—by next Wednesday. And congratulations, Casey," she added with a smile. "You're our cartoonist now!"

Ellie Lane looked up from her reading as Case sat down. "Let me see," she mouthed. He handed the comic to her. She bent over it for a couple of minutes, then looked up at him, her face serious. "It's funny," she whispered.

"It is?"

"Can I see?" the boy sitting behind Case asked softly. Case knew his name was Bryan, but he had never heard him speak before. The three of them sat in the quiet corner of the classroom. Some teachers at Ben Franklin seated their students alphabetically, and some had their own seating methods. They usually put the noisiest kids up front, Case noticed. But some teachers, like Ms. Yardley, let their students sit wherever they wanted. The funny thing was, they never changed seats once they sat down the first day.

Case had noticed something else that was strange: In the three classes he had where kids chose their own seats, the most popular kids sat in the back, the joker in class always sat at one side, on the aisle, the same kind of kid always sat in the front row, and there was always one quiet corner. *His* corner, except it wasn't so quiet all of a sudden.

"Casey, I'm going to have to ask you to put the comic away for now," Ms. Yardley said, trotting over to his seat. "Everyone's going to want to see it, but they will, soon enough." She had the attention of the entire class. Even the girls in the last row had stopped tossing their hair back while they pretended to read.

Everyone was looking at Case: He felt as though he was coming into focus at Ben Franklin for the first time, under their eyes—and all from one measly comic.

But at least it had happened. Case sat up a little straighter and pretended he wasn't surprised.

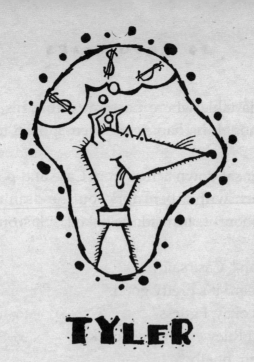

TYLER

As far as Case could tell, Tyler Thibault was the most popular kid in sixth grade. He was in Case's homeroom class: "It's *Tee*-bow," he had informed Ms. Riley the first time she took roll. Most of the other kids in class already knew who he was, though. Tyler was tall, thin, and strong. Everyone said he was good at sports, especially baseball. To Case, Tyler looked as if he was all points: pointed nose, pointed ears, even pointed eyebrows. Everyone noticed what he wore and reported what he said. Now he was walking up to the cafeteria table where Case sat eating his lunch, even though he had never even spoken to Case before.

Tyler sat down across from Case and poked at his lunch with a bent fork, but he didn't say a word about it. Instead, he asked, "So you did a comic?"

"Yeah," Case said.

"I heard it's pretty good."

"It's okay, I guess."

"Did Riley ever give it back?"

"Yeah, finally."

"I want to see it," Tyler announced. Then, quickly, he changed the subject. "Who's that guy you come to school with?" he asked as he finished his apple juice with a slurp.

"Huh?" Case asked, stalling. He carefully finished his milk and crumpled up his lunch sack. Someone dropped a tray, and a few kids howled and clapped.

"You know," Tyler said, without turning around. "That skinny guy with the glasses."

"Oh. Ned? He's—he's kind of a neighbor. So we ride the bus together, that's all."

"Why's he always go around smiling, anyway?"

"I don't know. I never noticed. He does that?"

"Yeah—it's like he's in his own little world."

Case suddenly remembered a summer conversation he'd had with Ned about the kids Case would be meeting at his new school. Ned said they probably wouldn't bother Case any, since they were all in their own little world. It was weird that Tyler would use those same words about Ned. *Maybe everybody at this school is in a different world*, Case thought. *Maybe Ben Franklin is like this giant solar system, and...*

"Hey!" Tyler said sharply. "So what about him?"

"Didn't you guys go to the same elementary school?"

"No, I went to Betsy Ross," Tyler said impatiently, as if stating a well-known fact. "Where'd *you* go, anyway?" he asked suddenly.

This was exactly what Case had been dreading ever since school had started, questions about his past. He wished he could disappear into the steamy funk that filled the cafeteria. "It was in New Jersey," he said cautiously.

"That where you learned to draw?" Tyler jumped from one subject to another like a TV cop asking questions. Case felt like a suspect about to be trapped, but a small part of him was happy everyone could see Tyler Thibault talking to him for so long. Around them, the clang and clatter of the cafeteria filled Case's ears. A nearby table of girls leaned together and giggled. One of them looked his way as she bit into a potato chip. The fragrance of long-cooked vegetables and mystery meat mingled with the smell of detergent and wax. Two teachers leaned against a far wall, sipping coffee from plastic cups, ignoring the surrounding chaos.

"I—uh, I guess so. A little. Not cartoons, though. I taught myself that."

"What's the comic for?"

"English. Yardley. We're doing a newspaper."

"I have Brill. You're lucky—Yardley's easy."

"She doesn't seem so easy," Case protested weakly.

"You get to do newspapers. We have to do worksheets in Brill's class. Every day. It's like having a test all the time. No homework, though."

"That's too bad," Case said. "I mean, that's good about the homework."

"So you going to do the comic for that newspaper?"

"Yeah. Yardley approved it. Everyone in my English class will get a copy."

"Bring it to homeroom again. I want to see the next one, too."

"Okay," Case said, hoping he would be able to hide *Dog Years* from Ms. Riley while Tyler inspected it.

"We could copy the comics and sell them, probably," Tyler was saying, starting to get excited. He raised an eyebrow, looked at Case, and waited.

"Sell them?"

"Yeah, maybe for a quarter apiece. You could get half. We'd each get half. It would be easy to photocopy. A dime a copy."

"This place I heard of does it for five cents," Case began, but Tyler didn't seem to hear him. He was busy making plans. He tapped his fork rapidly against the side of his green plastic tray and jiggled one leg. Suddenly the tapping and jiggling stopped.

"There's that guy," Tyler said. Case's head jerked up: Ned stood at the edge of the big crowded room, smiling and looking around. Someone bumped into him, and the things on his tray slid off. Tyler whistled softly and started tapping his fork again, like the secret conductor of the cafeteria. He looked thoughtful. "You sure you're not friends with him?"

"Why?" Case asked.

"I don't know. There's just something about him. And my dad says we're judged by the company we keep." He gestured toward Ned. When Ned had bent over to pick up his milk carton and lunch sack, his glasses had fallen off. No one even bothered to jeer at him.

Case ducked his head again, embarrassed for Ned and, at the same time, afraid his friend would notice him sitting there. "I'm going," he said to Tyler.

"Before he sees you?" Tyler asked, smiling.

"No. There's some stuff I have to do. *Really*," Case said. He had slipped out of the cafeteria by the time Ned found a seat at the end of a long, empty table.

Case's mother worked every Saturday in the old bookstore a couple of blocks away. Lily spent Saturday mornings with Mrs. Arnold, her baby-sitter, while Case worked at Mrs. Donovan's antique shop. At lunchtime, Case walked to Mrs. Arnold's house and took Lily home. He took care of Lily on Saturday afternoons.

Usually Case swept floors at the antique shop or stomped empty boxes flat for recycling, but that morning he had gotten to decorate the store's front window. He moved a stained-glass window filled with an artful design of wild birds from a rear storage room to the back of the display window. Case wanted more people to see the bird window.

When he left the shop at noon, someone had already been standing in front of the window, chuckling: Case had taken three of Lily's stuffed toy cats out of the apartment at the last minute that morning, and now they crouched at the base of the bird window. A person could almost see the cats' nylon whiskers quiver with excitement! Case thought Mrs. Donovan was pleased, and he was in a good mood.

Case and Ned spent most of Saturday afternoon together working on *Dog Years* at Case's kitchen table. Ned had brought over a pencil, eraser, ruler, and pen. He liked his own lettering tools best. "No offense, Case," he said, "but Lily chews on all your pencils, and she drew a happy face on the eraser. It's *distracting*."

Case decided that he and Ned should work on

several comic strips at once, but the two boys were also baby-sitting Lily that afternoon, and that made everything harder. Lily was quiet for the moment, sitting on the faded red linoleum floor, playing pick-up-sticks, and singing under her breath.

"I can't draw this stupid dog the same way in the different strips," Case complained. "It's harder than I thought. Don't you think this looks like a whole different dog?" He passed the second comic to Ned.

Ned stared at it. "I think maybe it's his ears. This one looks a little like a cow. And his spots are different than in the first strip."

"I have to make his *spots* the same, at least. I can't just hang a sign around the dog's neck with his name on it every week."

"You could if it was a dog tag, maybe. What *is* his name, anyway?" Ned asked.

"I don't even know. I keep coming up with different ones..." Case's voice trailed off.

"That's easy, Case," said Lily, interrupting her own little song. "His name is Spotty."

Case looked down at her. "Spotty? Isn't that a little too obvious, Lily? Hey, you moved that pick-up-stick."

"So what?" she asked.

"Well, you're not supposed to wiggle the other sticks when you pick one up. That's the whole point."

"Who says? It's my game." Cranky, Lily scrambled all the sticks with both hands. "Oh no, I moved a stick!" she yelled, glaring at her brother. Ned looked nervous. He didn't have any little brothers or sisters.

Case turned back to his work. With a howl, Lily jumped up, kicked at the pick-up-sticks, and ran into the bathroom. Case said, "She just wants attention."

"Maybe we should give it to her," Ned suggested.

"Later. We have to get busy or we won't finish."

"But what if we have to use the bathroom?" Ned asked, fidgeting in his seat.

"You need to?"

"Well, no, not yet. But I might later." Ned liked to plan ahead.

Case shrugged. "We can always go downstairs. Buddy's home, and he'll let us use his bathroom. He said he wants to see these first few comic strips anyway. So it'll all work out."

Ned turned slowly back to his lettering. "What's Lily doing in there, anyway?" he asked.

"Probably taking a nap. She makes a nest in the bathtub sometimes. She's kind of goofy lately. Maybe it's because she's so old. According to her, she's forty-two now."

"Huh?"

"It's a long story," Case said. After a few minutes, he looked up and tapped his chin thoughtfully with his pencil. "But you know," he said, "I think Lily was right about that name. It's obvious, but obvious can be good. Okay, from now on it's official: The dog's called Spotty."

"Maybe someday this dog will be as famous as Snoopy," said Ned, eyes shining. "This could be a historic moment!"

"Where our fortunes all began," Case said, laughing.

"Where we became millionaires."

"Zillionaires!!"

Lily's voice echoed against bathroom tiles as she yelled, "Stop laughing out there! And you better not be playing with my pick-up-sticks!"

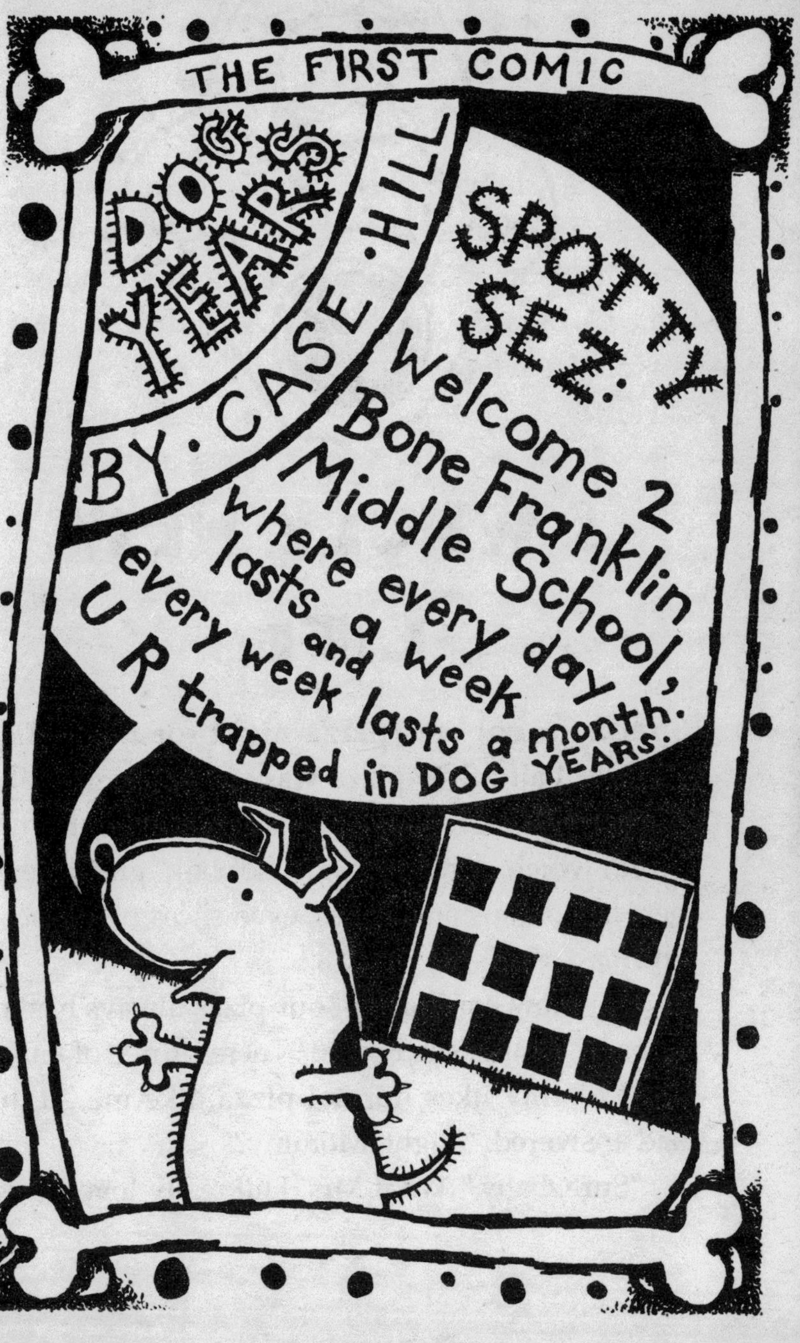
THE FIRST COMIC
DOG YEARS
BY · CASE · HILL
SPOTTY SEZ:
Welcome 2 Bone Franklin Middle School, where every day lasts a week and every week lasts a month. U R trapped in DOG YEARS.

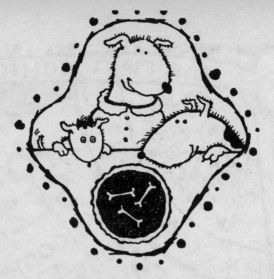

A WHOLE NEW LIFE

Sunday night was pizza night for the Hills. Usually, half of the pizza was plain cheese—Lily insisted on that. She hated all "green stuff" on pizza, which, for her, meant not only green peppers but onions and olives, even slices of pepperoni.

"But how come *half* of our pizza always has to be bare?" Case asked once. "There's three of us."

"Mommy likes normal pizza, like me," Lily had answered. "Right, Mommy?"

"Sure, baby." What Mrs. Hill really loved was

white pizza with broccoli and garlic, but she knew better than to suggest it.

The Hills's pizza passed its first close inspection that night, but partway through the meal, Lily's face darkened with suspicion. Case and his mother held their breath. "Hey, wait a minute. If we're eating pizza, that means it's Sunday, right?" Her mother nodded. Case dreaded Lily's next question, which followed immediately: "Well, if it's Sunday, how come Daddy hasn't called yet? He always calls on pizza night."

Dennis Hill's Sunday calls had become part of their new life in the city. The week before, Lily had answered the phone. She had been playing with her dolls in the big squashy chair, and she bounced and bounced in the chair as she talked, scattering tiny vinyl boots and sparkling capes. Eventually she had said, "Casey, Daddy wants you!" and handed him the phone. Then she had sat there, holding a doll and staring up at her brother.

"So, Case. How's things?"

"Okay, Dad."

"Lily told me someone yelled at you on the bus. That right?"

"Well, there was this crazy guy..."

"...because I don't want you taking any guff," Case's father had said. "It's okay to be respectful, but people have to earn it from you. I don't want people walking all over any son of mine, just because his dad's not there."

"They don't, Dad."

"Because a lot of fathers can't be around, Case. It's not just me. Fathers travel, get divorced, whatever. Life happens."

"I know, Dad."

"So, you doing any sports?"

"Well, in P.E. we do some track. Like running."

"I know what track is, Case. What about teams? You on any teams, like football?"

"I'm not big enough, and besides, you have to go to all this stuff after school. Practice, and games, and everything."

"And you have to baby-sit, right?" Case's dad said, his voice full of sarcasm.

"No, but I got this job—"

"You should be doing sports, Case. If I were there, you'd be doing sports."

"You still working out, Dad?" asked Case, trying to change the subject. He remembered how strong his father had looked the last time they'd visited him.

"You have to, around here. Keeps you from going nuts. You ought to try it, Case. Get strong, learn how to fight. If necessary."

"I guess," Case said as he twisted the telephone cord. Lily stared at him, solemn, and twisted her doll's long yellow hair.

"And listen," Dennis Hill continued. "You still kicking around with that kid? The one who lives with his granny?"

"Ned? Why?" Case asked, stalling.

"Answer me, mister."

"Yes, sir," Case said. "We're still friends. Why?" he asked again.

"You need to hang around some guys with regular families, that's all. Just because I'm not there doesn't mean you have to spend your time baby-sitting, sweeping out stores, and visiting grannies."

Case felt as if he were sinking through the floor. He wanted to scream *Yes, it* does *mean I have to do those things. It's all your fault!* But he couldn't speak.

"Case?" You still there?" his father demanded.

"I'm here, Dad."

"Well, put your mother on. I can see I'm not getting anywhere with you right now. Just don't forget you still have a father, and don't forget what I said."

Like I could, Case thought, as he beckoned his mother to the phone with a violent gesture.

His mother's conversation had lasted only a minute. "Right," she said. "Right. Okay, Dennis. Yes, I'll send it along. I'll remember. Okay, right. 'Bye." Then pizza night had begun.

Tonight was different, though. "I guess he just couldn't call for some reason, Lily," Mrs. Hill said.

"But why? He *always* calls on pizza night."

"Maybe someone else was using the phone. He'll probably call tomorrow."

"But he likes to call Sunday, to start our week off right," Lily said, her little chin wobbling.

Yeah, with a bang, Case thought, as he chose the biggest slice of pizza he could find and nipped off the pointed end.

"Couldn't we call him?" Lily asked, poking at some cheese.

"No, honey. We can't call in. But Lily, don't worry. He probably got very busy with something, that's all."

"Maybe he's sick," Case said.

"Oh, Case, for heaven's sake!" Mrs. Hill said, throwing down her napkin.

"Sick!" Lily whispered, pizza forgotten.

"He's not sick," her mother said.

"But what if he is?" Lily asked. "Would the judge tell us?"

"The judge isn't even there, Lily," Case began.

"Can't we go see Daddy?" Lily interrupted. "We better go see him! Buddy can drive."

"Lily, it isn't time for visiting now, and your father asked me to bring you two only on family visiting days. We're going again the weekend before Thanksgiving."

"But who's going to take care of him? He's sick. He needs us!"

"We don't know that, baby," Mrs. Hill said, with a quick scowl in Case's direction.

"But there has to be a reason Daddy didn't call..." Lily's voice trailed off.

"You're right, there's a reason for everything, Lily. We just don't happen to know what it is yet."

Lily frowned, not completely satisfied with this response. She looked down at her plain pizza slice and poked again at the cooling cheese. "This white stuff looks icky," she said. "Can't they make pizza with *nothing* on it?"

"Yeah, they do," Case said. "But they call it bread." After that, the Hills finished their supper in silence.

"Mom, why *do* you think Dad didn't call us tonight?" Case was tucked into his bed, and the striped curtains were pulled shut. His mother sat cross-legged at the end of the bed, leaning against the wall. She held a mug of tea. The green light from Case's clock radio glowed softly on her face.

She shrugged. "He'll call again soon, Case."

"But why not tonight?"

"I don't know. Maybe he was running out of things to say. He doesn't really know what's going on with us here anymore."

"Yeah, sometimes he acts like he thinks we're still in Cherry Hill. Things sure are different since we moved."

"This is a whole new life we're all leading," his mother agreed. Case was silent. "You do like it here, don't you, honey?" she asked, turning to face him.

"It's okay," Case said.

"You miss Cherry Hill?"

"I miss our house. I miss having my own room." The Hills had lived in a big house with three bedrooms and two bathrooms. There had been a swing set, a skateboard ramp, and a covered sandbox in their backyard, next to Mrs. Hill's vegetable garden. "I miss having another bathroom," Case added.

"Especially with Lily locking herself in ours all the time!" his mother laughed. "What else do you miss, Case? You miss all your old friends?"

Case sighed. He couldn't speak. His mom thought he had all these friends. Why did parents like to think their kids were so popular, he wondered. He had really only had two friends he thought were good ones. Three, counting Jeremy, but Jeremy moved away right before the trial. That left Paul and Tony.

Paul's mother had told him to stop seeing Case until after the trial. Tony, on the other hand, suddenly hadn't wanted to talk about anything *but* Case's father and the trial. It was as though Case himself had simply disappeared for Tony, who had wanted to be the big expert. He wanted to be the one to tell the other kids what was going on.

So Case had stopped talking to both Paul and Tony, but he couldn't tell his mother why. It was too complicated to explain, and anyway, it would just make her sad. "Nope," he said now. "I don't miss them."

"Because I'm sure you could still get together, honey. Cherry Hill's not that far."

"It seems like it's a million miles away," Case said.

She sighed and stretched. "I guess you're right."

Case tried to think of something else to say. "I liked it before you got a job. I miss you being home all the time, like after school."

"You do?"

"Yeah. There was all this good food and everything."

"I actually cooked then," she laughed. "Now we just throw things together."

"It's okay," Case said.

"Well, I'm glad you have some good memories about the old days, Case. Lily's too young to remember much, I guess."

"She can barely remember yesterday," Case agreed. "I guess that's why she keeps talking about Dad all the time," he added, suddenly understanding his little sister better. "She's afraid she'll forget him like she does everything else."

"I suppose," his mother said. She looked sad.

"I remember lots of things," Case went on. "Like when we all went to that mini golf place, and when Dad built me that skateboard ramp. And I remember going to the shore all the time. Me and Lily and you and Dad."

"We had some fun," his mother agreed.

"We were like everyone else, then," said Case. "Just like a regular family."

"I don't know about that, honey. To be honest, your father was probably breaking the law even then. We just didn't know. I didn't *want* to know, maybe."

"But how could you not know?" Case blurted out, suddenly angry. "You were married to him!"

His mother twisted her wedding ring. "Oh, Case, it's hard to explain. We hadn't been that close, not for years—long before there was any trouble with the law. I was so wrapped up with you two kids, and then my folks got sick, and your father—he was busy with his work. His regular job. That's what I thought, anyway. I didn't ask too many questions."

"So you mean that whole time I thought we

were happy, we really weren't?"

"No, I don't mean that. If you were happy, then you were happy," his mother corrected him. "You can't change that later. I was happy too, most of the time. I'm just saying it wasn't all perfect, even then. Before it happened." Mrs. Hill sipped the last of her tea.

"Is it better now?"

"You mean are we happier now? I don't think Lily is, poor thing. *I* feel happier, but how *you* feel is up to you to figure out."

Case thought for a minute. "I guess I'm happier about some things. I like being in a city, where nobody knows who you are."

"That's something, anyway."

"And I like working at Mrs. Donovan's."

"I like working too, even though I'm so tired sometimes I can hardly see straight. It's been so long since I had a job, I was really afraid I couldn't do it. It was almost like starting the first day of school, I was so nervous. Not that it's all that great, in terms of money. To tell the truth, we couldn't get by on what I earn now without the money I got from selling the house. Thank goodness my folks had owned it free and clear."

"We're okay though, aren't we, Mom? About money?"

Mrs. Hill squeezed her son's foot. "We're fine, Case. I'm getting back into the swing of things. I'm even going to take a computer class, did I tell you? Two afternoons a week. That will mean a raise, eventually."

"Where's the class?"

"This place not far from Ben Franklin, as a matter of fact. The bookstore is giving me time off from work. And speaking of school, how's it going for you, Case? You like it?"

"I like it okay. So far, at least," Case continued. "I mean it's uglier than my old school. There's no grass or trees at Ben Franklin. And everything's old there, compared to Cherry Hill. I hate riding the bus, too. It takes so long, and it's always crowded in the morning. Usually we can't even sit down! But the classes at Ben Franklin are more interesting. The kids have something to say, at least."

"Well, that's good news, anyway." Case's mother stood up, stretched again, and leaned over to kiss him good night. "Sleep tight, Case," she said.

After his mother had left, Case rolled over and pulled the covers up over his head like a hood. *And,* he thought, grim, *I like it when Dad doesn't call on Sundays. Sorry, Lily, but that's the truth, the whole truth, and nothing but the truth.*

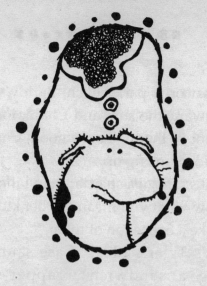

SORT OF A FRIEND

It was the first Saturday in October, warm in the sun despite a damp wind that blew off the river. Case and Buddy Haynes were sitting in Front Street Park, looking at the first finished comic strips. Buddy was a writer and had promised Case his honest opinion about *Dog Years*. A quiet, powerful man, Buddy had sat in a wheelchair for half his thirty-eight years. Long ago, he'd been in a car accident. Case almost didn't see the wheelchair anymore, he was so used to it.

Case sat on a park bench, Buddy's chair was turned toward the sun, and Champion stretched out in front of them. "Looks good, Case," Buddy finally said, glancing up.

"Thanks. This was harder than I thought."

"I know what you mean. I'll bet kids will save these, make a collection of them."

"That's Tyler's idea," Case said gloomily, watching a sandwich wrapper blow by. Champion lifted his head a moment and sniffed, then flopped over onto his side.

"Who's Tyler?" Buddy asked. "A new friend at school?"

"Sort of a friend, but not yet. Not really. He's this guy in my homeroom. He's pretty popular. I think he's even going to run for sixth-grade president—the elections are in a couple of weeks. Ellie says he'll run. She's the political expert. Tyler will probably win it. Then we'll *never* be friends."

"Sounds like maybe Ellie should run."

"She doesn't want to. Anyway, she says she wouldn't have a chance, that it's the leftover popular kids from fifth grade who win elections the first year in middle school."

"And that's Tyler. But he likes the comic?"

"Yeah, and he's got plans. He thinks we should photocopy and sell the strips and split the profits."

"'We' as in you and Ned?"

"Ned?" Case asked, frowning. "No, 'we' as in me and Tyler."

"Why is Tyler cutting himself in on this? He's not doing any of the work."

"Well, selling the strip was his idea, and he'd probably be the one to make the copies," Case explained. "And he knows the most people."

"And what about Ned?"

"What about him?"

"Doesn't Tyler think Ned should get some reward for his work on the comic?"

"I guess Tyler doesn't actually know Ned is working on it. I—I didn't get a chance to tell him yet."

Buddy looked carefully at the comics. "Ned's name isn't on these anywhere, Case. Isn't he your partner?"

"No. We decided he's more like my secret assistant."

"'We' as in you and Ned?" Buddy asked again.

"Right," Case said, starting to feel grouchy. "It's okay with Ned."

"Fine! Then it's certainly okay with me. Just be careful, Case."

"What do you mean, be careful? What of?"

"Oh, lots of things. Messing with your friends, for one."

"Tyler's my friend too—at least he could be."

"But it would be hard for you to say no to Tyler, right?" Buddy asked, as if thinking aloud.

"Oh, I could say no to him," Case said, not sure he really could.

"Good. But another thing. You know that saying, 'Give credit where credit is due'? You better do that."

"You mean with Ned and the lettering?" Buddy nodded. "But it's *my* class project," Case objected. "I'm doing all the drawing and writing. And what would I tell Ms. Yardley? Ned isn't even in her class."

"Is Tyler?"

"Well, no," Case admitted.

"Your teacher would probably understand

having a not-so-secret technical assistant. Lots of cartoonists have letterers."

"I'll think about it. But I don't think Ned even cares."

"Well, that's probably the biggest thing to be careful of, Case—Ned."

"Why? You think he's going to want more credit someday?"

Buddy looked at Case hard, then shrugged. "He may, but I doubt it. Ned's the type of guy who doesn't ask for much, even from a friend."

"That's good, isn't it?" Case asked.

"For him or for you?"

Case kicked angrily at a few wet leaves under his feet. "I don't get it. What do you mean?"

"Okay, Case, here it is, straight. I mean it sounds like you're kind of using Ned. He's your friend, don't forget."

"I can make new friends and still keep Ned," Case said, his voice icy. "In fact, I thought you told me how great it was I'd meet tons of kids at my new school. Now one kid almost likes me, *finally*, and you're all critical." Case jumped up from the park bench. "I have to get back home."

Champion got to his feet, swayed, and gave a squeaky yawn. For once, they didn't laugh at the dog's performance. "Wait a minute," Buddy said. "We'll go with you."

"No! I'm in a hurry," Case said, blushing. Silently, Buddy handed the comic strips back to Case. "Uh, well, I'll see you," Case said, miserable but still angry. "Thanks for looking at these."

"They're *really* good, Case. Maybe I forgot to say that."

"It doesn't matter."

"Well, good luck with it all."

"Yeah, thanks. It'll probably go okay," Case said. He reached out and stroked Champion's beautiful white fur. The big dog looked worried.

"You coming by the apartment to take Champion for his run this afternoon?" Buddy asked.

"Uh, I can't. I have to do something for my mom." There was a long silence between them.

"Well, soon, I hope," Buddy said. "Champion will be there, waiting for you. Don't forget." Buddy's voice was quiet.

"I won't," Case said. He turned and walked swiftly toward home, afraid to look back.

* * * * *

Case gave the comic to Tyler during home-room on Tuesday, along with two dollars for photocopying. "Good—that'll give us forty copies," Tyler said, pocketing the money.

"Uh, Tyler," Case said, "shouldn't you put in two dollars too, since we're partners?"

"Yeah, but we don't need eighty copies," Tyler pointed out. "Not yet, anyway."

"Then we should each put in just a dollar," Case said, feeling uneasy. He worked hard for his money at Mrs. Donovan's shop and wanted things to be fair.

"Look, Case," Tyler said patiently. "I'm saving for the class election. I have to buy poster board, markers, and everything."

"But, Tyler—"

"Hey, I didn't want to bring this up," Tyler said, "but I'm really doing all the work here. I have to get the copies made. And I'm the one passing out all the free copies."

"Huh? What free copies?"

"At lunch on Friday, after the newspaper comes out in your English class. That's the most important part of the plan. I give the comics to some friends of mine and to some older guys.

Then everyone will want to start buying it, so they can have one too. That's when we start making money. If we sell all twenty of the comics that are left for a quarter apiece, that'll be five bucks we can split. Two-fifty each."

"Yeah, but first we have to subtract the two bucks I just gave you," Case objected. "I get that back."

"No, that's our start-up cost," Tyler said. "Otherwise, we would just be getting a buck-fifty each for all that work. I can't do it for that. And I'm the one who knows the right guys to give *Dog Years* to in the first place. Without them, no one else will want it." Tyler was getting huffy.

"Okay, okay," Case soothed him. "I guess I see what you mean."

"Anyway, this is just for now," Tyler said. "Just until we get started. We can work something else out later, when *Dog Years* gets really popular. But my dad says you have to spend money to make money."

"Yeah, but it's my money we're spending," Case muttered as Tyler walked away.

Tyler gave the comic strip back in homeroom

on Wednesday morning. "There was tax, but I paid it," he said.

All the kids in Case's English class handed their revised assignments in on time that day. The articles on school politics, sports, and social events joined pages of jokes and craft ideas. Some kids had gotten Ms. Yardley's permission to work together on articles. Others were going to help their teacher copy and assemble the newspaper. The first installment of *Dog Years* went on top of the pile.

It was Friday, finally, the day Case had been waiting for. The newspaper would be handed out in English class. Case didn't know whether to feel excited or sick. But as soon as he looked in the bathroom mirror that morning, he knew. "Of all the days for my face to break out!"

"I thought only teenagers got zits," Lily said as she squinted over a bowl of cereal at her brother's face. Case's hand flew to his forehead, where the three bumps had appeared overnight. "Am I going to get zits?" she persisted, staring at Case's forehead as if she were hypnotized.

"Only if you live long enough," Case said,

shoving his cereal bowl away.

"Casey, I hardly think that was necessary," his mother said. "And, Lily, you know better than to make such personal remarks."

"I was only asking questions," Lily said. "It's good to ask questions, I thought."

"Not rude ones," Mrs. Hill said. "Now both of you, eat up, or we're all going to be late. And, Lily, maybe you should apologize to your big brother."

Lily looked up. A dribble of milk crept down her chin. "I'm sorry you have pimples, Case," she said sweetly.

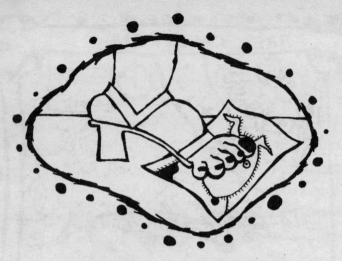

NOT GOOD ENOUGH

Case watched in horror as a photocopy of *Dog Years* floated from Tyler's notebook to Ms. Riley's big feet as she finished reading the daily bulletin. The homeroom teacher didn't see where it came from. She scooped up the paper and read it intently. The whole class was silent.

"Mr. Hill. My desk, please." Case stood up slowly and walked the short distance. She pointed dramatically at *Dog Years*.

"It's my comic for English class," Case said.

"I know what it is, Mr. Hill. I thought I told you I didn't need any more disruptions in my class." Case couldn't think of anything to say, so he remained silent. "Well?" Ms. Riley asked, tapping her foot. "Help me out here, Mr. Hill."

But I didn't bring it, Case thought wildly, glancing for a second at Tyler. Tyler was twisting a pencil back and forth, back and forth, and didn't look at Case.

Case forced himself to look back at Ms. Riley. "I'm sorry," he said simply.

"Sorry's not good enough, not in middle school," Ms. Riley said. "I'm tired of you kids always trying to get away with things behind my back. You were already warned once. I'm going to have to confiscate this. That means I keep it. I'll give it back on Monday," she said, her face softening a little. Sometimes she acted nice right after she had been extra-mean, as if she hoped the kids in her class would only remember the nice part.

Case realized Ms. Riley thought the comic she was holding was the one Case had to turn in. She thought that was the only copy, and she would keep it even if it was! There were forty copies altogether. Picturing his original assignment already safe in Ms. Yardley's hands, and thinking especially of the other thirty-nine copies in Tyler's notebook, Case could feel himself starting to grin.

He couldn't help it. He knew it was exactly the wrong thing to do, but the more he tried to stop, the wider his nervous smile grew. Case ducked his head, but he was sure Ms. Riley could see his expression. Out of the corner of his eye, Case spotted Tyler raising his notebook to cover his own grin.

"Is something funny, Mr. Hill?" Ms. Riley asked in a quiet, stony tone.

Case tried to speak calmly. "No," he said. He forced himself to meet her gaze and was shocked by the expression on her face. She looked like an angry little girl about to get even.

She glanced down at the comic, then raised her eyes slowly. She stared directly at the red bumps on Case's forehead. "I can see why you call him Spotty," she said in a hard, clear voice.

*   *   *   *   *

Ms. Yardley handed out the newspapers to

her students at the end of English class. Each of them looked first at what he or she had written for the paper, but then they all turned back to the first page, where *Dog Years* was displayed at the top. The room filled with whispers as they read the comic. "You did this whole thing?" Bryan asked Case. "Cool!"

"I like it," Ellie agreed, pulling her long hair back into an imaginary ponytail, then letting it drop in a shiny fan across the back of her blue sweater. A couple of kids Case hadn't gotten to know yet smiled at him on their way out the door.

By early afternoon, it was obvious that Tyler's plan was working. He had handed out most of the free copies in the cafeteria. Case was so nervous, he couldn't swallow a bite. His name was on the comic, but not many kids at the school knew who he was. Case had the feeling they were talking about him, though.

The kids who got a copy of the comic read it carefully, and some of them laughed. Others wanted to see it, and copies were passed around. Two or three were left behind on the sticky cafeteria tables, but they were quickly picked up and tucked into backpacks. Things couldn't have gone better, Case thought.

Case called Tyler that night. It was the first time he had ever done that. "How'd we do?" Case asked, after Tyler's father had called him to the phone.

"Not bad. I only sold twelve copies, but that's pretty good for the first day."

"So we made three bucks?"

"Yeah, in quarters. A buck-fifty each so far. Not bad," Tyler repeated. "We're looking good!"

Except he was still fifty cents behind where he was a week ago, Case thought, remembering the two dollars he'd given Tyler as start-up money.

"Remember, it takes money to make money," Tyler said, as if reading Case's mind.

"Are you going to try to sell the rest?"

"Sure. It may slow down a little next week, but once people get the idea the comic's coming out every Friday, they'll get into it and bring extra money to school. You want to try and sell a few?"

"I—I don't think I'd be very good at it," Case said. "I don't know that many people."

"No, probably not," Tyler said, matter-of-factly. "Hey, I have to hang up. My dad's expecting an important call."

"Okay," Case said, "I just wanted to know how everything went." He felt funny, as though he should apologize for even bothering Tyler.

"That's all right. I'll give you your share of the money Monday, before homeroom. I'm going to need two more bucks for copying, though, but we can settle up then. Unless you want to wait until the end of next week."

"No, Monday's good," Case said hastily. "Monday will be great. Well, good-bye," he added, remembering the important call Tyler's father was waiting for. "See you."

"Who were you talking with, Case?" his mother asked, looking up from her book. She was curled up on the sofa under a soft green blanket.

"This kid from school. We have homeroom together."

"That's nice. Is he a friend?"

Case considered for a moment. "Not exactly, not yet. We're kind of working on a project together."

"A school project?"

"Sort of." Case didn't know how to describe it to his mother. She loved *Dog Years*, but he knew she would find something wrong with selling it.

"Sort of a school project?" his mother teased. Case could tell she wanted him to talk to her about it.

"Mom, it's not that big a deal," Case said, his voice rising. "Can't I even use the phone? We never have any privacy around here!"

"Casey, of course you can use the phone! It's just—I don't know. It's only that you didn't sound like yourself when you were talking to him, whoever he was."

"Well, I *am* myself. In fact, today has been my best day at Ben Franklin so far. Don't you want me to be happy?"

"You certainly don't sound happy, Case," his mother said in a mild voice.

"Yes, I do. Or I did before you went and ruined everything!" he shouted.

Case stomped into the bathroom and shut the

door firmly, not quite slamming it. Only Lily slammed doors, when she was having a tantrum, he told himself. All he needed was a little privacy. Was that so much to ask? And he *was* happy. Things were going great for him. *Finally.*

RIPPED OFF?

The next day was Saturday, and Marge Donovan, the owner of the antique shop where Case worked, was thrilled. "Casey Hill, I must have had a dozen people walk into the store last week because of your window display! The stuffed animals were an inspiration. None of the customers bought the stained glass, but I made a few other sales."

"That's great," Case said, smiling.

"Well, all the credit goes to you. Now I have a

challenge for you," Mrs. Donovan went on. "It's already the second Saturday in October. I've decided I want you to do a special Halloween window for me, using things from the shop. I'd need it set up by next Saturday at the latest. Can you do it?"

"Sure!" Case said, pleased and excited. It wouldn't be any harder than doing all those *Dog Years*, he thought, and it was a whole lot better than just cleaning up around the shop. That made him remember his father's sarcastic words about baby-sitting, sweeping floors, and visiting grannies. His dad thought working in a shop was dumb, boring. Not tough enough. Case felt some of his confidence drain away. "I mean, I *think* I can do it," he said.

"You can spend the whole of next week on it, starting today," Mrs. Donovan continued, "and I'll give you a budget of twenty-five dollars for any special decorations you might need. Ribbons, paper, that sort of thing. And there will be an extra twenty-five dollars for you, when it's done."

"Okay," Case said, trying not to look surprised. *Twenty-five dollars! This is great*, he thought, as he explored dusty shelves in the big storeroom. He and Ned had finished a bunch of comics already, and they didn't need to start working on the next ones for a while, so there was plenty of time for him to work on the Halloween window.

He thought back to the lucky night the summer before when he first met Mrs. Donovan. A policeman had accused him of stealing a Chinese bowl she'd thrown away in her trash. "It's his, fair and square, officer," she'd said, coming to his rescue. She talked to Case that night about the bowl, her shop, and its front window, which Case had seen. He discovered she knew his mother slightly, and Buddy Haynes, too.

Mrs. Donovan had recognized Case's interest in art right away and offered him a part-time job in her shop. But this was the first time she'd ever given him extra money to work with, and time away from his usual chores at the shop. Thoughts of his father, his mother, Lily, Ms. Riley, Tyler,

Ned—all of Case's worries faded away as he planned the shop's Halloween window.

"Mrs. Donovan?" Case asked, when they finally settled back for a break late that morning. She made strong black coffee for herself and gave Case one of the cartons of orange juice she always kept on hand for him.

"Hmm?" She sipped her coffee, eyes half closed.

"Did you ever get ripped off?"

"Ripped off?"

"Did anybody ever try to cheat you, I mean."

"Oh, sure, Casey. Lots of times. Probably even some times I don't know about, if they were successful at it!"

"Oh, yeah. I guess not."

"Why? Did someone cheat you out of something?"

"I'm not sure. I mean, do you always know when it's happening? Can you always tell?"

"Sometimes you have a feeling right away, I think, even if you're not sure. But you have to be careful. I can think of any number of times I thought someone was trying to take advantage of me, here in the shop, and it turned out I was wrong."

"You were wrong?" Case was surprised Mrs. Donovan could make a mistake about anything. She always seemed so sure of herself. All grown-ups did. But first his mom had told him that when she started her new job she felt like a kid starting a new school, and now Mrs. Donovan was telling him she made mistakes. And she didn't even seem to care much! He had always thought someday, when he grew up, he would feel sure about things. Like his dad did.

Just then, a familiar screech filled the shop's still air. "Those are mine!" It was Lily. Case's mother had gotten her from the sitter, and they had come by the shop for Case. They were going out for lunch.

"Lily, keep your voice down," Mrs. Hill said. "I'm sure they just look like yours. Sorry, Marge," she added, turning to her friend.

"But they *are* mine," Lily insisted. "Tiger Annie, Growlers, Mr. Fluff—oh, there you are," she crooned. "I want them back!" she roared suddenly.

Mrs. Hill looked at the stuffed animals in the window. "They *do* look familiar," she said, frowning. "Case?"

"I just borrowed them for a couple of weeks," Case said, uneasy.

"Without asking?" Mrs. Donovan and his mother said together.

"You guys had already left for the sitter when I had the idea," Case explained. "I couldn't ask."

Case's little sister had kicked her sneakers off and was starting to climb into the display. The stained-glass window swayed. Mrs. Hill grabbed Lily's legs and held them tight. "Don't you move an inch," she warned.

"I'll get the cats for you," Case said. "Hang on." He carefully retrieved the three stuffed animals. The wild birds pictured in the stained-glass window looked lonely without them.

Lily looked sideways at Mrs. Donovan and her mother, to make sure they were watching her. She liked lots of sympathy. "Oh, come on," Case said, disgusted. "It's not like you even knew they were gone, Lily. You have more stuffed animals than any kid I know." It was true. Lily had so many stuffed animals she sometimes slept on the floor, just to give them all room in bed.

"I knew they were gone, I really knew. I just wasn't saying anything," Lily said, clutching all three to her chest. "My heart was broken."

"Well, maybe you can squeeze out a tear or two while you're at it," Case said.

Lily did better than that—she burst out crying. "You didn't even ask me!" she sobbed.

"That's enough, you two," Mrs. Hill said. "Casey, Lily is right. You should have asked permission, or at least told her what you'd done."

"She would have said no," Case said.

"You should give your sister a little more credit," Mrs. Hill said.

"I would have said yes!" Lily buried her face in the stuffed animals' shiny fur. "Probably."

"And, Lily," her mother went on, "you're just crying to hear yourself cry. If you kept your animal collection tidy, you'd have known three of them had wandered off."

"They didn't wander, they were kidnapped!" Lily said.

"Or *kitty*-napped," Mrs. Donovan said, smiling.

"And he never even thanked me or anything," Lily finished with a sniff. "He wanted everybody to think it was all him."

"Thanks," Case said gruffly.

"Too late!"

"In any event," their mother said, "if you two want lunch, we're going to leave now. I have to be back at work by two. I'm sure Marge here will be sorry to see us go, but..."

They all filed out the door in silence, which was very rare for Lily and a little unusual for Mrs. Hill and Case. Tiger Annie, Growlers, and Mr. Fluff had never been much for talking, though.

FRIENDS AGAIN

The Hills ate pita-bread sandwiches at the Greek restaurant near the bookstore where Mrs. Hill worked. After lunch the three of them stood on the busy sidewalk for a moment and talked.

"I'll be home around five tonight," Mrs. Hill said. "Case, you be sure and take that chicken out of the freezer as soon as you get home, before you and Lily go downstairs to Buddy's."

"To Buddy's?" Case asked in dismay. He hadn't seen Buddy or Champion in almost a week, ever since their talk in the park about Ned. Usually Case took Champion for a run two or three nights a week, right after dinner. Buddy, in his wheelchair, couldn't run with the big dog. Sometimes, before getting back to his homework, Case had stayed to talk with Buddy. But Case had been avoiding their neighbor all week long. *Buddy is the one who should be embarrassed*, Case thought angrily, *after saying all that stuff in the park.*

Case's mother said, "Champion needs some exercise, and so do you kids. Buddy's finishing up a project and can't get out today, so I told him you and Lily would take the dog out for a nice long walk."

"Yes, yes, yes!" Lily squealed, hopping up and down while holding her stuffed animals tight.

"Mom," Case moaned, "that's not fair. You shouldn't have told him that. What if I had plans?"

His mother glanced at her watch, in a hurry to return to work. "Case, don't be silly. Buddy's your friend, after all. You baby-sit Lily every Saturday afternoon—what plans could you have? It's a beautiful day, and Buddy could use some help. I said you'd be there by three."

"Mom!"

"That's enough. We'll talk about this later. 'Bye, Lily—give me a hug, baby. Don't forget about the chicken, Case, or we'll be having drumstick Popsicles for dinner."

"Yeah, okay," Case said with a sigh. He trudged off toward their apartment, holding Lily's sticky hand. She skipped all the way.

All too soon it was three o'clock. "Case, come *on*," Lily said, eager to see Champion again.

"I'm coming, I'm coming." They clattered down the wooden stairs to the little hallway below. Lily knocked on Buddy's door.

"We're here!" she called out. The door swung open. Case smelled coffee brewing and heard the printer to Buddy's computer beeping and whirring. Champion crouched playfully, the leash in his mouth. Case tried to avoid looking at Buddy.

But Buddy didn't seem to notice. "Thanks," he said. "I should get this finished up in the next hour. Well, I *have* to—a messenger is coming by for it at four. But I picked up some brownies at the bakery, so we can all celebrate when you get back."

"I don't know—" Case began.

"Brownies! My favorite!" Lily said.

"I thought chocolate cake was your favorite," Case said grouchily.

"Anything that's part of the chocolate family tree is my favorite," Lily said, hugging Champion. The dog shook his leash, and Case attached it to the heavy collar. Finally, he looked at Buddy. Buddy smiled, and all of a sudden Case felt a little more cheerful.

Maybe staying for brownies wouldn't be so bad, he thought, as Champion pulled them out the door.

In fact, the brownies were great, especially with the cold milk Buddy poured for them all. Case gulped down a whole glassful as Champion lapped noisily at his big bowl of water. They were all thirsty. Lily arranged the brownies on a blue plate, nibbling loose crumbs from her fingers.

"Hey, don't slobber all over them," Case said, wiping a milk moustache off with his sleeve.

"I'm not slobbering," Lily said, as a crumb fell from the corner of her mouth. Champion looked hopeful as Lily carefully carried the plate to Buddy's table.

"Don't even think about it," Buddy warned his dog. Case smiled. Champion sighed, turned around three times, then lay down in a sunny spot on the rug.

"Did you finish your work?" Case asked, shy with Buddy after having been angry all week long. Buddy nodded. Lily finished her brownie, licked every finger, and curled up on the floor next to Champion. She rested her head against the big dog's side. Champion gave her a loving sniff, then stretched out and went to sleep.

"Good deal—you wore them both out," Buddy said with a grin.

Case drank his second glass of milk more slowly and wondered what they were going to talk about. Not *Dog Years* or Ned, that was for sure.

But Buddy was speaking. "I saw that display window you did over at Marge Donovan's shop. I liked it."

"Yeah, thanks. She did, too. Those were Lily's stuffed animals," he added quickly.

"Marge told me she was going to ask you to do a special Halloween window."

"Huh?" Case said. He didn't like the idea of them talking about him.

"You going to do it?"

"I guess. It'll be fun, kind of. But I have to do the whole thing this week. She's going to give me money for supplies and pay me extra, too. I'm trying to save for Christmas," Case added.

"You have any ideas for the window yet?"

"I think I got a good one. Did you ever see that little canoe back in the corner of the storeroom?"

"It's half-size, right? Made out of birch bark?"

Case nodded. "I guess some guy made it as a hobby a long time ago," he said, quickly losing his shyness. "But it's perfect for what I want to do. I need to figure out how to make it look like it's floating in water, though."

"Water, hmm..." Buddy said, thinking. "You know, over on Arch Street there's this little paper shop. Near the flag store, you know?" Case nodded. "They carry unusual things. They had big rolls of paper in the window last week, and one roll was dark blue with little gold flecks. That would look good, I think."

"Like water?"

"You could crumple it up and surround the

canoe with it. Why don't you go take a look after school on Monday?"

"Okay," Case said. "It'd probably take all the supply money, but I wouldn't need to buy anything else. Everything else I need for the display is in the shop already."

"Well, you tell me if you need any help with the window, okay?"

"Thanks," Case said slowly. "I think I *will* need help setting up the window on Thursday, after school. You working then?"

"I'll be working with you," Buddy said, smiling. "The artistic paper crumpler, that's me! I've had lots of practice. Just look in my wastebasket!"

"Thanks, Buddy," Case said.

"Hey, it's nothing."

No it isn't, it's something, Case thought, as he washed the blue plate and milk glasses. He was glad things were getting back to normal. They were friends again.

"Your father telephoned me at work this afternoon," Case's mother said that night after she had put Lily to bed.

"He did? At work? Why?"

Mrs. Hill chose her words carefully. "He

wanted to tell me he's not going to call you kids for a while. He says it's too hard."

"Hard on who?"

"He didn't specify."

"But what about Lily? She really needs to talk to him, Mom."

"I know, Case. And what about you?"

"Me too, I guess. But it's harder for Lily. What are you going to tell her?"

"We'll still be seeing him on family days. There's one coming up pretty soon."

"That's something, anyway," Case said. "I don't think it will help her much, though." It was a long time before Case spoke again. "How come, Mom?" he asked finally.

"Oh, Case," she said. "I don't want to make excuses for your father, but it can't be easy for him to figure out what his role in the family is anymore. He's so out of touch. And it must be hard enough for him, just being in prison."

"It's his own fault," Case said.

"You're right, but we're all stuck with the consequences. I think it'll take a while for us to sort it out, especially Lily. But it can't be easy for your father," she repeated. "There must be a lot of questions in his head."

"He never seems to have *any* questions when he talks to me," Case said, "only answers. He acts like nobody else could ever be right about anything. I think he's just being selfish, not calling."

"Who knows?" his mother said. It sounded as though her voice was coming from far away as she added, "I hate to say it, but I'm a little relieved he isn't calling tomorrow night. It will make Sunday a lot nicer. For me, anyway, and maybe for you."

THAT TERRIBLE WEEK

The entire next week was a disaster for Case. He came early to homeroom on Monday, ready to collect his dollar-fifty from Tyler. But Tyler didn't show up until the last minute, and he was surrounded by his friends, as usual. One of them, Lorenzo, looked at Case and snickered. Lorenzo was short and neat. He always wore clothes that were much too big, but he did it on purpose, and his clothes were always spotless. Case thought Lorenzo was like Tyler's very clean shadow. Case tried to get Tyler's attention, but Tyler was too busy to look at him.

Case finally caught up with Tyler in the hall after fifth period. "Hey, I need that money from selling the comic. You were going to bring it, remember?"

"Yeah," Tyler said, "but you're going to have to add fifty cents to it so we can print twenty more copies to sell this week. You got fifty cents on you, Case?"

Case did, but it was to buy a snack after school. He didn't want to hand his snack money over to Tyler. Instead, he took a deep breath and asked, "Why don't *you* pay the fifty cents?"

Tyler shrugged and frowned. "I could, I guess. It's kind of hard with the election coming up and everything, but..."

"I still think you should pay the fifty cents," Case said again.

"Okay," Tyler finally said. "I'll donate fifty cents, and that'll give us two bucks, enough for twenty copies of this week's *Dog Years*. But I have to have the comic tomorrow, don't forget."

"Yeah, and I need it back Wednesday to turn it

in on time, don't *you* forget."

Tyler nodded, grinned, and was gone, followed closely by a laughing Lorenzo.

He had finally gotten Tyler to pay for something, Case thought, pleased, as he slammed his locker shut. It wasn't until he took his seat in English class that he remembered Tyler had kept the dollar-fifty Case had been waiting to collect. Now he had paid out three-fifty for printing, and he hadn't gotten one penny back. *I'm a jerk*, he thought. *I really* am *getting ripped off.*

Tuesday, Case forgot his bus pass and had to pay cash. Both to and from school.

Wednesday was another bad day. Case almost turned the comic in late, thanks to Tyler, who hadn't even brought it with him to homeroom. Instead, Tyler dashed into Case's English class right before it started and, to Ms. Yardley's surprise, tossed the comic onto her desk. Then he ran out the door.

"Casey," Ms. Yardley asked, "what was all that about?"

"Oh—oh, that was just some kid who wanted to see *Dog Years*, since he's not in the class," Case said. He was furious with Tyler, though. What if the comic had been lost or hadn't been turned in on time? Everyone's project had to be handed in promptly and in perfect condition for the class newspaper to be printed by Friday.

Thursday was even worse than Wednesday. Something happened at lunch that Case knew he'd never forget. He had taken a seat next to Bryan, from English. Ellie walked by, hesitated, then sat with them. "So is Tyler going to win it?" Bryan asked Ellie, as she neatly folded the paper from her straw into little squares.

"Unless there's an upset," she confirmed.

"You going to vote for him?" Case asked her, hoping she would answer "No."

"*I* am," Bryan said, leaning forward over the table. "Sure. He's going to win anyway."

"I am *not* voting for him," Ellie said. "I'd write in Mickey Mouse's name first, but luckily I don't have to. Katy's running." But before she could go on, Bryan made a face at her.

A second later, Case felt a tap on his shoulder. He turned around and there stood Tyler, Lorenzo, and a couple of other kids Case had seen around but didn't know. To Case's surprise, Ned was with them. Tyler and Ned were both smiling, but the two smiles were different. Ned didn't look happy. Tyler did. Lorenzo stood right behind Tyler, as usual, and he looked happiest of all.

"Hey, Case," Tyler said, ignoring Bryan and Ellie completely, "this kid is saying he works on *Dog Years* with you. I heard him telling a guy I know that it's him who really does all the lettering."

Somehow, Case swallowed the bite of sandwich he'd been chewing. He was afraid they could all hear the pounding of his heart. *He* sure could. Then he looked at Ned and thought maybe it was Ned's heart he heard pounding. He looked away.

"*Dog Years* is mine," Case began. He honestly didn't know what he would say next.

"That's what I thought," Tyler said, satisfied. He gave Ned a little shove with his bony shoulder. "I told you," he said to the others who stood around, watching and grinning. "Case barely even knows this kid. He told me so a couple of weeks ago."

Case couldn't help but look up at Ned again. Ned's smile wavered, and he blinked two or three times, fast. Then he smiled at Case again, turned, and walked away. Case almost hated Ned for that last smile.

"Pathetic," Tyler announced. "I told him he better shut up about it, too, or he'd really be sorry."

"Yeah," Lorenzo said. "Lying about stuff. Taking credit for stuff he never did. Pathetic," he echoed.

"*Dog Years* belongs to me and Case," Tyler continued. "Right, Case?"

After a moment Case nodded, but he couldn't speak. He couldn't finish his lunch, either. He remained quiet all afternoon, even as he and Buddy set up the special Halloween window display at Marge Donovan's shop.

That terrible week didn't end there. On Friday, there was an excited stir at the end of English class as Ms. Yardley passed out the second issue of the class newspaper. *Dog Years* was at the top of the first page again. Case felt a poke between his shoulder blades. "Looks good, Case," Bryan said.

"Thanks, Bry."

But Ms. Yardley had something else to say. She called him to her desk. She looked worried;

even her curls seemed to droop. "Casey, Mr. Nava has asked us to come into his office after class. It's my free period then."

"Mr. Nava?" Case asked, confused.

"The assistant principal."

"But—but I can't. I have Spanish!"

Ms. Yardley almost looked as though she was going to smile for a moment. The bell rang. "He'll write you an excuse. Don't worry about *that*." Ellie and Bry stared curiously at Case as he followed Ms. Yardley from the class.

The school offices were near the big doors Case entered each morning, but he'd never really noticed them before. He and Ms. Yardley sat down in a big waiting room. Case stared up at a poster telling him not to take drugs. A secretary smiled and waggled her fingers at Ms. Yardley, then returned to her work.

"Casey," the English teacher said softly, "do you know the reason we're here?"

"The class newspaper?" Case guessed.

"Probably, but I'm not sure why, exactly. I got the project okayed." Ms. Yardley chewed on a thumbnail. Case was surprised to see his teacher nervous, and he started to feel scared.

"Maybe Ms. Riley turned us in! I have her for

homeroom. I don't think she likes the idea of *Dog Years* very much."

Ms. Yardley smiled a little. "You have Ms. Riley?" she asked, raising an eyebrow. "She said something about the paper to me a couple of weeks ago, in the lounge. I'm pretty sure that's not it, though."

A door opened. A tall man in a dark suit and red tie looked out and beckoned them into his office. The chairs in the office were more comfortable than the ones in the waiting room, and there was carpet on the floor. "Ms. Yardley," he greeted the English teacher with a nod as she and Case sat for a second time.

"Mr. Nava, this is Casey Hill," Ms. Yardley said.

"Casey, I've seen your *Dog Years* comic in Ms. Yardley's paper. Very humorous," he said, frowning.

Great, Case thought. Mr. Nava looked like he hadn't laughed in ten years.

Mr. Nava was still speaking. "You show a great deal of talent, Casey."

"Thank you," Case croaked. Ms. Yardley waited, silent, but at least she wasn't chewing her fingernails anymore. She was sitting up even straighter than usual, though.

"But there's a problem," Mr. Nava continued. "A concerned parent phoned in. Seems her son had a copy of *Dog Years.* Not the whole newspaper, just the comic. But he's an eighth grader, obviously not in Ms. Yardley's sixth-grade English class."

Ms. Yardley frowned, confused.

Mr. Nava continued. "This eighth grader told his mother he'd bought the comic for a quarter during lunch. That's what she objected to—kids selling things on campus. Not a good idea, Casey, for obvious reasons. It's against school policy, in fact."

Ms. Yardley turned to Case. "Do you know anything about this?" she asked.

"I—yeah, I guess so," Case said. But he was wondering why Tyler wasn't there. This was all *his* bright idea! How come *he* never got in trouble?

"You *guess* so?" Mr. Nava asked, narrowing his eyes at Case.

"I mean, I *know* so. It was—sold to some kids. Last week. Maybe the new one will be too, later on today."

"Maybe?" Ms. Yardley asked quickly. "That means you don't know for sure, and that means someone else is involved. Who?"

Case's mind raced, but he was silent.

"Was it that boy who ran into my classroom with the comic on Wednesday?" Ms. Yardley asked.

Still Case didn't speak. He was afraid to look at his teacher.

"Do you have anything at all to contribute here, Casey?" Mr. Nava asked.

"No, except I didn't know it was against school policy to sell stuff," Case said. "And Ms. Yardley didn't know anything about *Dog Years* being for sale."

"I assumed not," Mr. Nava said. Then he pushed his big chair back from the desk and sighed. "I'll tell you what. There will be no more sales on campus. You get the word out today, Casey, to whomever. Before lunch." Case nodded. Mr. Nava turned to Ms. Yardley and said, "I don't think any real harm has been done. I think we can just write this episode off to Casey's being unfamiliar with our rules. I feel confident the newspaper is still a sound project, Ms. Yardley."

"My students are really getting involved in it," she said. She looked at Case intently. "Do you understand about not selling copies of the comic on campus?"

"I understand."

Mr. Nava stood up and finally smiled at him. His face looked as if it was trying out something new. "I'll get a late slip for you, Casey," he said. "And thanks for your time, Ms. Yardley."

"Well, I'm glad to find out what's been going on."

"Nothing too serious," Mr. Nava said, smoothing back his hair. "No real harm done, as long as we nip this thing in the bud."

Case scowled as he waited for the paper that would admit him late to Spanish. "*Adiós*, Tyler," he muttered, as he walked down the empty hallway toward his class.

DOING TIME

That night, in Case's dream, Ms. Riley lectured her homeroom class. "Mr. Hill has been wasting the taxpayers' money, doodling his time away," she said. "Furthermore, *Dog Ears* makes fun of our school. 'Bone Franklin,' indeed."

"No!" Case said, jumping to his feet. "I'm not making fun of the school. I'm making fun of what it's like to be a kid. And it's *Dog YEARS*, not *Dog EARS*."

"Are you telling me I can't read?" Ms. Riley began, scowling.

"Of course not! I just—"

"Because if you are, you're in deep trouble, Mr. Hill. Not that you're a stranger to trouble."

Ms. Riley turned to the rest of her homeroom students and spoke: "I think you should know that Mr. Hill has spent time in prison. Right here in Philadelphia, at the Southwark Penitentiary. It seems Mr. Hill takes things that belong to other people."

"No!" Case shouted for a second time, turning to face the others. Tyler Thibault grinned at him in surprise. "It wasn't me—it's my father. *He's* the one in prison." Immediately, he was sorry he had spoken.

The boy who sat behind Case stared at him. "Your dad was in prison?" he asked, pity in his voice.

"He still is," Case said.

"And that's another waste of the taxpayers' money," Ms. Riley said flatly.

"Like father, like son," Tyler said, sitting up

straight. "That's what *my* dad always says, anyhow."

Case didn't want to hear any more about Tyler's father or his constant sayings. "Shut up," he said to him. "Your dad's not right about everything."

"Well, at least he's not doing time in jail," Tyler said.

Case turned to Ms. Riley, furious. He wanted to get even with Tyler for saying that. "Tyler's the one who's been selling *Dog Years*. Go ahead and tell Mr. Nava! And Tyler owes me money, too." He whirled to face Tyler again. "At least my father pays his debts!"

"That's enough," Ms. Riley said. "I'm just trying to do a job here, and being a referee isn't part of it. Mr. Nava will take care of this. Case, follow me."

"But what about Tyler?" Case cried as she walked out the door.

The dream continued. Case trailed after his teacher as she climbed up one steep flight of stairs, then down the stairs, up another flight, then down again. Finally they were in Mr. Nava's waiting room. The secretary waved them into his office.

Ms. Yardley, Ned, Ellie, and Bryan sat on a long bench facing Mr. Nava's desk. Buddy, in his wheelchair, sat with Champion at the end of the bench. Champion looked sternly at Case.

"Jury," Mr. Nava said, "Case has been violating school policy."

"News that doesn't amaze me one little bit," Ms. Riley said loudly. "He tried to make me look like a fool in front of the whole class." After a pause, she added, "Sorry, Mr. Hill." She looked as if she hoped her "sorry" would make up for her harsh words.

It didn't. Case ignored her. "Why am I on trial, anyway?" he asked Mr. Nava. "I didn't do anything wrong."

Ms. Yardley stood up. "I think we should give Case the benefit of the doubt, Mr. Nava. He's a good boy."

"But is he popular?" Mr. Nava asked. "Tyler Thibault," he said, turning to the door, "come in, please." Tyler entered, followed closely by

Lorenzo. They stood in front of Mr. Nava's desk. "Tyler," Mr. Nava asked, "you're popular, you would know. Is Casey violating school policy?"

"Uh, I guess so, sir," Tyler said.

"I guess so," Lorenzo echoed. His immaculate white sneakers seemed to blaze as he and Tyler walked to one side of the room and waited.

"Looking good, Lorenzo," Tyler said under his breath.

Mr. Nava turned to the English teacher. "Ms. Yardley, you know it's against the rules to be unpopular in middle school. We have a name for it: Sustained Unpopularity. And it's grounds for detention."

"But, Mr. Nava," Buddy said, wheeling himself forward, "Case has a lot of other good qualities."

"Like what?"

"He's nice," Ellie said. Bryan nodded.

"He hands his work in on time. Usually," Ms. Yardley said.

"And he's a good friend," said Buddy. "Just ask Ned, here. Ned?" Everyone turned to look at Ned.

"Ned?" said Mr. Nava. "Is Case a good friend?"

Ned stood up. He didn't look at Case, and he wasn't smiling. "I barely even know this kid," he said. "And I'm kind of busy with some stuff. Can I go now?"

In his dream, Case watched Ned leave the room. Somehow, he didn't feel at all surprised.

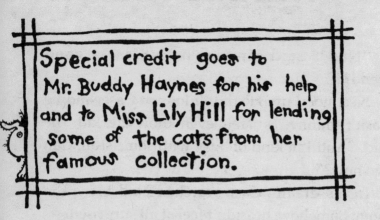

Special credit goes to Mr. Buddy Haynes for his help and to Miss Lily Hill for lending some of the cats from her famous collection.

CREDIT

The Halloween display window was finished, and everyone who looked at it that Saturday laughed. Buddy had torn the midnight-blue paper into long curvy strips and gently crumpled them into small waves. The paper darkened the window, but the tiny gold flecks in the paper glinted in the light.

The small white canoe was propped up and was riding through blue paper waves. Paddling the canoe were two ghosts. Case had made them from old linen tablecloths he'd found folded up in a chest.

"I'm glad you didn't cut holes in the cloth for their eyes," Mrs. Donovan said.

"No way. I wouldn't wreck those. Anyway, black paper circles show up better."

The old-fashioned gentleman ghost wore a top hat, and the lacy lady ghost wore a straw bonnet. Peeking over the side of the canoe were three furry passengers, Tiger Annie, Growlers, and Mr. Fluff. Each one of Lily's prized stuffed animals wore a little black Halloween mask.

In the corner of the window was a large, carefully lettered sign Case had made thanking Lily and Buddy for their help.

"It's a triumph," Mrs. Donovan said, giving Case a little hug as they stood on the sidewalk admiring the window. She usually wasn't very huggy, and none of his friends were around, so Case didn't mind. It had started to rain, but people stopped to look at the window anyway. Mrs. Donovan handed Case a gray envelope. "There's your pay for the week and the extra twenty-five dollars, too," she said.

"Thanks." Case stuffed the envelope into his jacket pocket as Champion ran up, towing Lily. Mrs. Hill and Buddy followed close behind.

Lily grinned her Halloween pumpkin smile as she looked at the sign in the window. "There's my name," she said, proud. "Read it to me, Case!"

As he read the sign to his little sister, Case was surprised at how much pleasure it gave her. Then, reluctantly, he found himself thinking of Ned, and how hard Ned had worked on *Dog Years.* No wonder he had told someone at school he had been part of the comic too! Case cringed as he thought of Ned's last smile in the cafeteria.

Lily read the sign aloud herself. She sighed happily. "'From her famous collection,'" she said. "It *is* famous. All over the world!"

"Oh, Case," his mother said, giving him a hug, "it looks great."

"You wouldn't believe the comments we got just yesterday," Mrs. Donovan said. "Oh, and someone's interested in buying the canoe! That's one thing I thought I'd never sell."

"They're not going to take it out of the window, are they?" Case asked, worried.

"Not until we're through with it," Mrs. Donovan reassured him.

"I think Tiger Annie, Growlers, and Mr. Fluff *like* being famous, don't you, kind of?" Lily asked.

Everyone laughed. Then Buddy said, "It's freezing out here. Let's head back to my place. Dinner should be about ready." Champion gave a happy bark and led the way home.

Buddy's apartment smelled wonderful as they all tumbled in from the cold street.

They piled their coats and jackets on a chair near his front door. Marge Donovan sniffed. "Chili, Buddy?"

"Two pots." Buddy smiled. "One spicy, one mild," he added, glancing at Lily.

"I want mine spicy!" Lily announced.

"And she means it," Mrs. Hill said with a laugh. Case hadn't seen his mom have so much fun in a long time; she had been avoiding her old Cherry Hill friends and had been too tired to do much with her new ones.

"You're not going to believe this, but I made dessert, too," Buddy said as they cleared the table after the long, noisy meal.

"I thought I smelled something baking," Mrs. Donovan said. "It's your famous apple pie, isn't it, Buddy?"

"It is," he said proudly.

"Hey, wait a minute," Lily said. "Is everything famous around here?"

"You bet," Buddy said, tousling her hair.

"Buddy," Case whispered when things had quieted down a little, "is it okay if I go upstairs for a couple of minutes? I have to make a phone call."

"You can call from down here, if you want. Or do you need privacy?" Buddy asked.

"Privacy."

"We'll hold dessert for you," Buddy said. "Take your time."

Case stepped into the front hall, closing Buddy's door softly behind him. It was cool and quiet after the laughter and warmth of Buddy's apartment. Case plodded up the stairs and unlocked his own front door. He took a deep breath, walked over to the phone, and dialed.

"Hello?" a shaky voice answered. It was Ned's grandmother.

"Hello, Mrs. Ryan? Is Ned there? It's Case."

"Oh, hello, Casey," she said, glad to hear his voice. "Neddy's up in his room. I'll just go get him. Hold on a minute, will you?"

Case waited a long time, stretching the telephone cord out as straight as it would go, then letting it bounce back. "Boing, boing," he whispered. He did it again. Finally, Mrs. Ryan returned to the phone.

"Casey?" she said, sounding a little confused, a little troubled. "Neddy can't come to the phone right now. He's...he's busy with something. Can he call you back later?"

"He said he wanted to call me back?" Case asked, hopeful.

"Well, no," Mrs. Ryan admitted. "He didn't exactly say that. I'm sure he'll want to, though."

"Thanks, Mrs. Ryan," Case said. He wasn't so sure Ned would *ever* call back.

Sunday night was hard for Lily, which meant it was a hard night for everyone. "But *why* can't Daddy call?" she asked for the third time.

"He *can* call, Lily. It's not that he can't," Mrs. Hill tried to explain. "He just wants to wait a while."

"For what? You're lying! He'd call if he could," Lily said, shoving her chair away from the kitchen table. Case watched milk slop over the side of his glass.

"Your father wants to wait for the family day visit, Lily. He thinks that would be better."

"But that's forever," Lily said, unbelieving.

"No, baby. Just a few more weeks."

"Forever!" Lily cried. "And don't call me 'baby.' I'm not your baby!"

"Lily, it's not Mom's fault," Case began.

His sister turned to face him. "You're right, it's *your* fault, Casey, for fighting with Daddy whenever he calls."

"I didn't fight with him!" Case said, indignant. "Maybe I should have," he added. "I'd fight with him about not calling, anyway, and making Mom be the one to tell you." Case pictured his father pumping iron while life fell apart for the rest of them. "He only thinks about himself."

"Shut up, shut up!" Lily shouted, clamping her hands over her ears and running toward the bathroom. "And leave my daddy alone!" The door slammed.

Case looked at his mother. "I'm sorry I said that," he mumbled in her direction.

"I'm not sure it's really true, Casey," she said faintly.

"Oh, it's true," Case said. "I'm just sorry I said it."

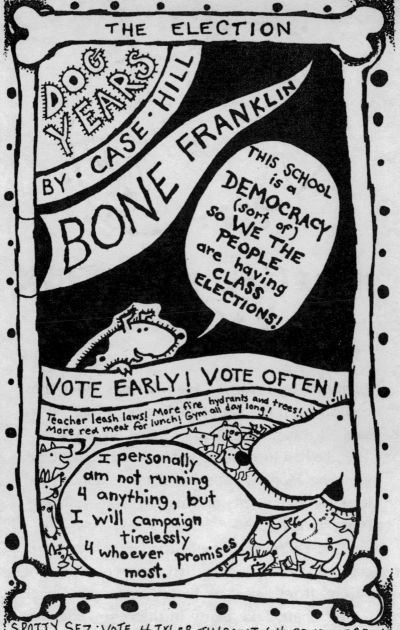

ILLEGAL ELECTION TACTICS

At lunch on Friday, Case had told Tyler they couldn't sell the comic anymore. "Fine," Tyler said. "I was getting tired of doing all the work." Then he had turned and left Case standing alone. Now, on Monday morning, Case was surprised to see so many kids reading *Dog Years* as homeroom started.

"Mr. Hill, what's this?" The entire homeroom class had been full of excited whispers a moment before. It fell silent as Ms. Riley towered over Case's chair. Like many in the room, she was holding a photocopy of the most recent *Dog Years*. Now Case glanced at Tyler, who grinned at him and shrugged. "Mr. Hill?" The comic rattled in the homeroom teacher's hand.

"It's my comic. But I can explain..."

"I don't *think* so, Mr. Hill. This is serious."

"I know," Case said, gloomy. "We weren't supposed to sell it."

"Sell it? You have got to be kidding, Mr. Hill," Ms. Riley sputtered. "Anyway, I'm not talking about that. I'm talking about illegal election tactics."

Illegal? Election? Tactics? Case thought wildly. He knew what each word meant, but the three words together confused him.

"Don't play dumb with me," Ms. Riley continued, jabbing her finger into Case's chest. "I'm disappointed in you enough as it is." Then she jabbed her finger at the bottom of the comic. "It's all here in black-and-white. Not that I disapprove of the message," she added, tossing a toothy smile in Tyler's direction, "but we can't have you trying to rig the class election just because *you* want our friend Tyler to be president too."

"What do you mean?" Case asked, hoarse.

But Ms. Riley had a question of her own. "Just how dense do you think I am, Mr. Hill?"

Case couldn't answer that one, not without getting into even more trouble. Instead, he opened his notebook and looked at his own copy of the second *Dog Years*, the one Tyler had turned in late to Ms. Yardley. The one he, Case, had been too busy to look at carefully. Everything seemed all right, so why—Case gasped.

Neatly printed along the bottom of the comic was the message: "Spotty Sez: Vote 4 Tyler Thibault 6th Grade Prez." It wasn't Case's lettering, and it wasn't Ned's, either.

The bell rang, and kids left in a clatter for first period. Case heard a loud "Way to go, *Tee*-bow!" as Tyler pushed his way out the door with a whoop.

"Mr. Nava's office now, Mr. Hill," Ms. Riley said. She looked tired, as though she'd just fought in an arm-wrestling match. But Case was already out the door.

"Tyler!" he yelled down the crowded hall. Tyler was huddled with some friends near the drinking fountain, laughing and high-fiving.

Case stormed up to them. "Did you write that stuff in at the bottom of my comic?" he asked in a low voice. He didn't know what made him angrier, the election message or the thought of Tyler marking up *Dog Years*.

"Hey, calm down," Tyler said with a laugh. "It was *our* comic, and it turned out great! You'll be famous, Case."

"How many of them did you sell?" Case demanded.

"Sell? About—let's say five. So we're even on the money thing, Case," Tyler said, and he grinned. "Not to worry!" Lorenzo laughed and poked Tyler with his elbow.

"What about after lunch?" Case asked. "Did you keep on selling them after I told you not to?"

Tyler opened his eyes wide, innocent. "No, I promise. I didn't sell any after lunch. Hey, I've got to get to class. Got to keep my record clean if I'm going to win this election."

"You might win the election, but you're still a loser, Tyler," Case said, his voice hard. Tyler frowned, then he turned into the crowd and was gone.

Lorenzo said, "Hey, Tyler didn't *sell* any more election comics. But he gave away a couple hundred! Free publicity for *Dog Years.*"

"But, but—how could Tyler afford to just give the comic away?" Case sputtered. "Two hundred copies?"

Lorenzo laughed. "He could have given away a thousand, if he wanted. Tyler's dad owns the biggest chain of photocopy stores in Philadelphia. He doesn't have to pay for anything! Oh—and thanks for your campaign contributions, Case," he added.

"No, wait." Case gripped Lorenzo's sweatshirt as he turned to leave. "Now I'm in more trouble with Mr. Nava..."

"...and Tyler isn't in trouble at all," Lorenzo finished for him. He pulled away from Case's grip, looked down, and frowned at the wrinkle. "Anyway, his dad would kill him if he got in trouble. He wants Tyler to win this election, *bad*," he added. "He always says success has to start somewhere!" Lorenzo started to saunter down the hall.

"Hey, Lorenzo," Case called after him, "you're

the one who's pathetic, not Ned." Lorenzo froze, not turning around.

Case walked slowly in the other direction, to Mr. Nava's office. He knew the way this time.

THE NEW CASE

Mr. Nava, hands clasped behind his head, leaned back in his big chair. It creaked under his weight. "Well, Casey," he said finally. "Casey, Casey." Case looked up from an ink spot on the carpet and made himself meet the assistant principal's gaze. It seemed as though he had been sitting in that office for days. Years. Mr. Nava spoke again. "So you claim this was all your idea?"

Case blinked, thinking hard. He hadn't claimed anything, much less that. Was this a trick to get him to say someone else was involved too? Aloud, he said, "Well, I made up the comic myself."

Mr. Nava sighed. "I know that, Casey. And you sold it..." Case was silent. "...until I ordered you to stop selling it, that is. But you got around that, didn't you? You gave the comic away on campus, knowing it had a campaign message printed in it." Still, Case didn't speak. "Do you think that's fair to the girl who's running against Tyler Thibault? Shouldn't she get equal time?"

"I—I guess she should," Case said. He couldn't even remember her name.

"And don't you think it was a dirty trick to play on Ms. Yardley, sneaking in that message? Of course, she should have noticed it herself."

"It wasn't Ms. Yardley's fault," Case interrupted.

Mr. Nava looked doubtful but said, "At least you're not trying to shift the blame, here. It's obvious who's at fault. So what are we going to do about this, Casey? Call off the election, just because of you?"

A silence filled the office. Case tried to guess

what Mr. Nava wanted him to say. He wondered if this was a trick question. He finally asked, "Should I maybe apologize to the girl who's running against Tyler?"

"That might be a start."

"I guess I could do that in the next comic," Case said, hoping he wouldn't have to face her in person.

"There isn't going to be a 'next comic.' I thought that was understood."

"Uh, no, I guess not."

"Well, understand it now. I've decided to allow the class newspaper to continue, but *Dog Years* is history."

"Okay," Case said, miserable.

"Ms. Yardley tried to encourage you, and I tried to be a good sport about the comic, and we both gave you a break about the whole selling thing. And how did you repay us?" Again, Case didn't speak. "I know you're new here," Mr. Nava went on. "I know you admire Tyler—you just got carried away trying to impress him."

"I guess I did," Case said.

Mr. Nava's phone rang. "Yes?" he said. He listened for a moment, then said, "Thanks, I'll tell him." He hung up and turned to Case. "Casey,

I'm suspending you for the rest of the week. You'll miss voting in the election on Friday. I want everyone to know how serious I consider this, trying to influence an election and all. Your teachers have agreed to send down the week's assignments to the office so you won't fall too far behind. You can write a note to Katy Jefferson saying you're sorry, and turn it in with your homework. I'm adding an announcement to tomorrow's bulletin, apologizing to Katy, and to Tyler, too. This mess wasn't any favor to *him*, you know.

"Now, we called your mother to come get you," Mr. Nava continued.

"No!" Case said, really upset for the first time. "She's working. I can take the bus..."

"It's the middle of the morning. You don't just walk out the door. Someone has to pick you up."

"But my mom—" Case stopped, not wanting to tell this stranger how worried his mother had been ever since his dad's trial. He didn't want to tell Mr. Nava how upset she would be that Case had gotten into this much trouble.

"Hang on, Casey. Your mother can't come get you. The bookstore says she's at some computer training class in Center City. We called the next name on your emergency numbers list."

Case frowned, trying to remember. "Who—" he began.

"It's a Mr. Buddy Haynes. He's on his way, Casey."

As if sensing Case's mood, Buddy was quiet during the drive home. As for Case, he didn't think he could talk if he had to. He felt as if his throat were paralyzed, and he poked at it with cold fingers. Then he fiddled with the heater vents and stared out the window of the van. He had been suspended, he thought, but at least he hadn't blabbed everything to Mr. Nava!

Buddy parked near the house. Though it wasn't necessary, Case held the wheelchair steady as Buddy settled into it. A damp wind blew big wet leaves against the two of them as they headed home. Case finally spoke. "You mad?" he asked Buddy.

"At you? Naw," Buddy said.

"But I interrupted your writing and everything," Case said.

"Hey, the way it was going, I should give you a reward," Buddy said with a laugh. As they neared their door he added, "Look, it's almost lunch. You can go on upstairs if you really want, but why don't you come in for some soup? I promise I won't dump on you for what happened."

Case gave a feeble smile. "You mean it?"

Buddy nodded. "I figure you already got it pretty good from that Nava bird."

"Yeah, I did," Case said. But he guessed he had handled it okay...

"...Not that I knew Tyler had written the message on the comic," he found himself telling Buddy while eating his third bowl of homemade vegetable soup.

"But you didn't tell Nava that?"

"No."

"Why not?"

"I guess I figured if I was going to take all the credit, I might as well take all the blame," Case said.

"What about your English teacher? Did she know?"

"No, I didn't even see her today," Case said, and he groaned. "What if she thinks I tried to trick her on purpose?"

Buddy looked again at the comic. He shook his head. "It doesn't even look like the same lettering," he said finally.

"*None* of it's my lettering, for that matter," Case pointed out.

"But your English teacher will figure out you didn't write that message in," Buddy reassured Case, "even without knowing all the details. I don't know why Nava couldn't figure it out. He's got eyes."

"Well, it's all over now, except for telling Mom," Case said. "*Dog Years* is through. And you know the worst thing?"

"What's that?"

"It's not that I got ripped off, that's for sure. That just kind of snuck up on me. But the worst thing is that Tyler is going to get elected president now, partly thanks to *Dog Years*. Also, Ned never got any credit for working on the comic—not that he's even speaking to me. And not that I blame him."

Buddy looked curious but didn't ask any questions.

Case sighed, and Champion rested his heavy chin on Case's leg. "He feels sorry for me. Don't you, boy?" Case asked, scratching behind one of the dog's velvety ears.

Buddy laughed. "Hate to disappoint you, but I think he's just trying for the rest of that soup! Champion, down."

Champion walked slowly over to the window, made his three turns, and curled up, his tail hiding his nose. "No harm in trying, anyway," Case said.

"But you know what?" Buddy asked. "There *is* harm in giving up."

"What do you mean, giving up? It's not like there's anything I can do about anything."

"That's the old Case talking. I remember when you first moved here, how helpless you acted."

"I guess I *was* pretty helpless," Case said.

"Well, I think you've changed."

"You do?" Case thought a moment. "Maybe you're right. I got a job, I started Ben Franklin okay, and kids liked my comic. I even faced down Tyler and Lorenzo! Sort of, anyway."

"That's the new Case! And maybe you can even right a couple of wrongs. The election doesn't necessarily have to go to Tyler. You can get even."

Case smiled at that. "I'm glad Mom can't hear you. Revenge isn't a big thing with her. She says it just causes more problems. She'd probably tell me I deserve all the bad stuff that happened."

"Some of it, maybe," Buddy said with a laugh. "She's right about revenge, for the most part. But that's the good thing about being creative, Case. You don't have to just sit back and take things, you can come up with colorful ways of settling the score. Ways that even a mother could love."

"Like what?" Case asked, his interest growing.

"Like I'll tell you. The basic idea, anyway..."

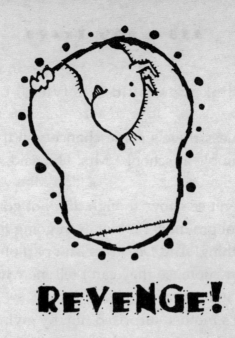

REVENGE!

Revenge! Case thought gleefully. Buddy could call it righting wrongs or getting even, or whatever, but it sure felt great.

Even his mother approved of the plan, once she heard a few details. "It's perfect, Casey," she said. "You're turning the tables on that weasel just right. He set himself up for this, and turnabout is fair play, as they say." She frowned as she brushed Lily's hair. Lily gave a little yip.

"I think we should kill Tyler," Lily said fiercely.

"I guess there's some chance you'll get into more trouble at school," Mrs. Hill said, ignoring Lily.

"I don't see how, though. I'm not going to be on school grounds. I'm not even going to be selling anything! And *Dog Years* isn't part of the class paper anymore, so they can't tell me what not to do with it. It belongs to me."

Case's mother surprised him by giving a little shrug and smiling. "Well," she said, "there's no point in going through life being afraid—or angry. This is a good response, in spite of Lily's thoughtful suggestion. And besides," she laughed, "that twerp has it coming! If you do get in trouble, I'll be there to back you up this time."

"That's funny," Case said. "That's what Buddy said, too."

"I still think I should have gone in to talk to Mr. Nava, to explain what really happened."

"No," Case said, thinking what his life would be like at Ben Franklin if he blamed everything on Tyler. "I have three whole years at that school, don't forget. At least Ms. Yardley kind of understands now."

"It was nice of her to call."

"Well, she *did* see Tyler turn the comic in late, and she could tell that stupid campaign message was in a different lettering, when she had time to really look at it."

"But *Dog Years* is still out of the class newspaper?" she asked.

"Until next January, anyway. But she's going to let me do that obituary column for the rest of the semester. I get to be 'Mr. Black' after all!" Case said, already planning his first entry.

"Case, you are *so weird*," his mother said. Case thought of Ned when he heard that word. He missed him.

"Me too!" Lily said. "I'm weird too, right?"

"Right—you're my little weirdos," Mrs. Hill said, hugging them tight. "Now put away your laundry, Mr. Black," his mother said. "And Lily, go pick up those stuffed animals."

"And then I'm going to help Case with his plan," Lily said.

"We all are," Mrs. Hill said, smiling at Case.

* * * * *

Everyone got into the act. Case drew the final comic, and Buddy did the lettering this time. He also contributed five dollars for printing. "This is an investment chance I don't want to miss," he told Case.

"It's an investment?"

"Sure—in taking some power back from the Tyler Thibaults of this world! And there are lots of them, believe me."

Case's mother insisted on donating another five dollars. "I want to be in on this, too," she said.

"Me, too!" Lily said. "Since we're not going to kill him, at least I get to do this. Take anything," she added grandly, pointing to the big pile of coins on her bed. Lily scrounged and saved every penny, so Case knew how much she really wanted to help.

"Okay, Lily," he said. "I'll take—a dollar?"

"A dollar?" she asked in a hushed voice. "But all I have is nickels and dimes and stuff."

"Well, how about if I take, um, six dimes and eight nickels?" Case asked, figuring it out fast. *Lily would be easy to cheat*, he thought.

She looked relieved. "Sure! I'll count it out."

Case left her counting and went down to Buddy's apartment.

"So with my five dollars and Lily's one dollar, that's a total of sixteen bucks," he told Buddy.

"And at five cents a copy, that'll give us three hundred twenty copies. You said there's five hundred kids in sixth grade at Ben Franklin?" Case nodded. "Or you could go for the bright paper colors at ten cents a copy," Buddy said. "It's up to you."

Case frowned, trying to think. "That'd be— one hundred sixty copies?" he asked. He thought some more, then decided. "Let's go for the color. I'm just trying to make a point, not wipe Tyler out. Anyway, I think *Dog Years* will look good on colored paper!"

"Kids will sure notice it more. Probably keep it longer, too."

"So where are we going to go for the printing?"

Buddy grinned. "There're lots of places we *could* go," he said, "but I kind of like the Thibault Copies chain. They have a store a few blocks away."

"In a way I hate to give them any business," Case said, thinking of the sixteen dollars. "But in another way..."

"...it's perfect," Buddy finished. "Let's go print, pal!"

They printed one hundred sixty final copies of *Dog Years* on lime green, turquoise, bright yellow, and glowing orange paper that Wednesday afternoon. The election was two days away.

The Hills and Buddy went out together Thursday morning. Champion stayed home, since they were taking the bus. Mrs. Hill took time off from work. "It's worth it," she said. "I don't want to miss a thing."

Buddy gave a stack of the comics to a friend of his who ran a video arcade near the school. After buying everyone a pretzel around the corner, Case's mother gave another stack of comics to the man who operated the stand. Lily licked mustard from her lips and said, "We should do this more often!"

Case left a big stack with the man who ran the newsstand next to the bus stop. The man's folding table, crammed with gum and candy, was like a magnet for the kids waiting for buses after school. "Casey, Casey, where you been?" the man asked, excited and worried. "My best customer," he explained, turning to Case's mother.

"Hmm," she said.

Case laughed. "I'm okay, Mr. Petroni. I'll be back next week. But do you think you could give these comics away? It has to be *today*," he added.

"You mean sell them?" Mr. Petroni asked.

"No, they're free."

"Sure, Casey, sure! It's pretty," he added, squinting at the comic. He cleared off some space and set the thick stack in the middle of the snack table. He put a rock on top so the comics wouldn't blow away.

"Thanks, Mr. Petroni," Case said. Lily nudged him, and he leaned over and listened to her whispered plea. He grinned and dug into his pocket. "Bubble gum for my helper and investor," he said, plunking two quarters on the table. Lily grinned her shy jack-o'-lantern smile, and Mr. Petroni smiled back, enchanted.

"What a beauty!" he said. "What a face! For

her, it's free bubble gum today. Keep your money, Case. It's an honor, believe me."

"What a nice man," Case's mother said as they boarded the bus, waving good-bye.

Lily nodded as she chewed the gum, her face still bright with pleasure. "I think he's about the *nicest* man I ever met."

"Feeling good about everything?" Buddy asked Case as the bus started to move.

"Yeah, we did it!"

"*You* did it, you mean. It was your drawing."

"And your lettering," Case said.

"Now, all we have to do is wait for school to get out," Buddy said. "I wonder if the comic will have any effect on the election tomorrow."

"You know what?" Case said. "It almost doesn't matter. At least I tried to make things right."

"Well, it's out of your hands now. All the copies of the comic are out there, out in the world."

"*Almost* all of them..." Case said.

He delivered the last copy of *Dog Years* alone. He walked to Ned's house, even though he knew

Ned was still at school. He rang the doorbell. An excited yapping started up at once behind Ned's front door. "It's just me, Lacy," Case called out, but the barking continued nonstop. After a long time, the door opened a crack. "Mrs. Ryan?" Case said.

"Casey! Neddy's not home yet. Did school get out early?"

"No, I didn't go today," Case explained. He handed the old woman a turquoise *Dog Years*. "Can you give this to Ned? I wanted to make sure he gets a copy."

"Of course," she said. "Lacy, get back!" She tried to hold the little black dog's sparkly collar so she could open the door wider. "Don't you want to come in and wait for him?"

"No, that's all right. I can't. I have to go work at Mrs. Donovan's. But I'll call Ned tomorrow. Tell him I'll call tomorrow, okay?" he repeated.

Mrs. Ryan nodded. "All right, Casey, I will. Back, Lacy, back!" she shouted like a lion tamer. She shut the door with a bang.

Friday morning, it was still dark outside when Case woke up. He peered at the lighted numbers on his clock: five-thirty. He was so nervous about the class election that day he couldn't sleep anymore. And he was going to miss the whole thing!

As the minutes crawled by, Case imagined Tyler getting up and preparing for his big day. Had he seen the latest comic? He cared so much about looking good; how would he look to the kids at Ben Franklin now? Would the comic make any difference? Case rolled over and thought about Tyler's father. He sounded weird. Was Tyler afraid of him?

Case imagined Lorenzo next. He pictured Lorenzo waking up and choosing what big clean clothes to wear that day. Why did Lorenzo care so much about how he looked, what he wore? Why did he care about being Tyler's friend, for that matter?

After breakfast, Mrs. Hill left for the day with Lily. "Now, remember," she told Case first, "no TV. This isn't a vacation."

"I know," he agreed. "There's lots of other stuff to do. Anyway, I'll probably go early to Mrs.

Donovan's shop. Maybe it will make the day go faster."

But it didn't. Case imagined he could hear every single bell at Ben Franklin as the morning went on, and on.

Friday night, the phone was ringing as the Hills walked in the door. Lily ran to answer it. "Case, it's some girl," she said, scowling.

Case grabbed the phone from her. "Hello?" he said.

"Hi, Case? It's Ellie. From English class?" It sounded like a question, but Case knew it wasn't.

"Oh, hi."

"You're the fourth Hill I called! I didn't have your phone number."

"You called three other people, just to find me?"

"Well," she said, sounding embarrassed, "I wanted to make sure you're okay and everything."

"I'm fine," he said. "I got suspended, though."

"I know. That's so dumb. Everybody knows

that wasn't your fault, what Tyler wrote in."

"Not everybody," Case said. "Mr. Nava didn't know."

"Oh, *him*. Anyway, when are you coming back?"

"Monday."

"You are? I heard you got suspended for the whole rest of the semester."

Case laughed. "No, just for this week."

"Oh. Well, everyone was wondering. That's all kids could talk about."

"Really?" Case asked, amazed.

"You know school. There's nothing else to do." They both laughed. "Anyway, everyone got all mad at Tyler when they heard you were suspended. So he got really worried and made Lorenzo tell everyone you had *too* written in the election message. He said you did it to impress him, to try and get in with his group."

"Did anyone believe it?"

"No way. Bryan and I told everyone that we saw Tyler run into English and turn in your comic that day. Everyone recognizes Tyler. We said anyway, just look at the lettering, it's all different. So Tyler ended up looking really stupid."

"Ned Ryan did the lettering," Case said.

"I know. I saw. I got a copy of the last comic after school at the pretzel stand yesterday. That was so great!"

"Thanks. So how did it go today?"

"Who knows? We won't find out until Monday. You'll be there for that, anyway."

"Yeah," Case said. "I will."

There was a pause. "I guess that's all," Ellie said.

"Thanks for calling me," Case said.

"That's okay. Well, see you."

"See you." Case hung up the phone.

Lily was still standing there, staring at him. "Who was that?" she demanded.

"Nobody," Case said. "It was a wrong number."

"Oh," Lily said. "Why didn't you say so?"

"I just did."

Later that night, when Lily was asleep and his mother was reading in her bedroom, Case took a deep breath, walked over to the phone, and dialed. Ned answered on the first ring. "Hello?"

"Hi, Ned?"

"Yeah. Is this Case?"

"Yeah."

"Are you all right? I heard you got suspended for the rest of the year."

"No, just the week. Everyone will probably be disappointed when I show up on Monday," Case said with a little laugh.

"Nah," Ned said, then added, "Hey, Case, thanks for—for saying that stuff in the comic yesterday."

"That's okay."

"Who did that lettering, anyway?" Ned asked, sounding a little jealous. "It was pretty good."

"Buddy did it. It was just a one-time thing, though. You're still the best letterer around."

"I'm okay, I guess."

"I just hope you don't get into any trouble about what I said," Case added.

"I hope I do," Ned said. "Maybe some of your fame will rub off on me!"

"I'm famous?"

"A *little* famous. Around school, anyway. For now, but Tuesday it'll probably be somebody else."

"Probably." Case took another deep breath and said, "Ned, I'm really sorry about what happened. About everything."

"That's okay, I guess," Ned mumbled. Case could tell he didn't want to talk about it. "I always said you'd make friends easier than me."

"Yeah, well... Look, you want to come over?" Case asked, changing the subject. "Spend the night? I'm sure it's okay with Mom."

There was a long pause, then Ned said, "I don't know. You know my granny."

"What about tomorrow, then?"

After another pause, Ned said, "Can I call you in the morning and say for sure?"

"I'll be working at Mrs. Donovan's until noon."

"I'll walk over there and tell you. I *might* be able to do it. I just—I just have to check and stuff."

Case knew Ned meant he had to think about it. "It's okay. See you tomorrow, I hope."

"Yeah, okay." Ned hesitated, then burst out laughing. "Tee-Bone! That was perfect, Case.

Everyone was grabbing a copy. I never thought I'd say this, but—I can't wait for school on Monday."

They hung up, and Case grinned as he stared again at his copy of the final *Dog Years*. Like Ned, he had never thought he'd say it, but he couldn't wait for school on Monday, either!

October 30

Dear Dad,

Hi! Well, it's Halloween tomorrow. Lily's going to be the tooth fairy, Mom made a costume. Ned is coming over. He's still my best friend. We're taking Lily out trick-or-treating. We're her bodyguards, Mom says. Ned is going to be the hole in the ozone layer, I don't know what I'll be yet. Maybe I'm too old. Things are okay at school. Homeroom stinks, but that's just 15 minutes. I can live through it. Mom says time goes by faster when you get older anyway, so that's good news. She is learning computers for work. Are you still working out? I go running sometimes with my neighbor's dog, but that's all. I'm pretty busy. Here are some comics for you I drew. They were for school, but I'm not doing any more for a while. We had a class election and now this girl named Katy Jefferson is 6th grade president. She's nice, I met her once. Pretty soon is family day, what do you want us to bring? Write and tell me, but write Lily first. Or I think you should call her, she needs you. I didn't get a letter from you yet but that's okay. Not much has been happening here either. I guess it's just one of those years.

Your son,

Case

Sally Warner is a widely exhibited artist and the author of two other books for young readers: *Ellie and the Bunheads* and *Some Friend*, the sequel to *Dog Years*. A teacher for many years, she now works full-time as a writer and an illustrator. *Dog Years*, her first book for Knopf, was inspired by her own early years as an artist, as well as her concern for the families of prisoners.

The mother of two grown sons, Ms. Warner lives in Pasadena, California.